WINDING

EVER

HIGHER

Amy Sutphin

A Twisted Realm Novella

To my sister Dena who
always supported me
I owe you a sweet tea

Chapter One

Before the sun had risen, Emya was roused and urged to dress by a harried maid. After laying out an outfit for Emya, she hurried out, muttering as she went. The sky was mute blue outside the window as the first rays of dawn began to peek over the horizon. With a sinking feeling, Emya remembered that she hadn't packed. Rising from the bed, she opened the closet. Empty. Frowning, she looked around the room for a packed bag. She found none.

The outfit the maid had laid out was her own, the one she'd been wearing the day she escaped, though it had been altered. The holes in the tunic and trousers were now patched with sturdy fabric, the stains had been worked out almost entirely, and a jacket of the same cloth as the patches now accompanied it. On the floor was a pair of well-made black leather boots. She dressed, wondering if Mrs. Mellia had changed her mind about giving her all those outfits. Lastly pulling on the boots she took a few paces around the room. Solid and snug, she felt as though she could walk to the ends of the world in them. Ready to go, she pulled open the drawer for her bag containing her matches, knife, and the Companion. Her heart stopped. The bag was gone. The drawer was empty.

Wrenching open the bedroom door, she ran through the halls, dodging the maids and ignoring their indignant calls. She burst into Felix's room. He stood by the bed, shirt half-buttoned, feet bare, his brow shot up in surprise.

"It's gone," she said, breathless not for the exertion, but fear. "My bag, with the object. It's gone."

He frowned, hurrying out the door without a word. Emya followed him down the stairs, ignoring the dirty looks they got. She noted how the maids didn't seem brave enough to scold Felix as they did her. In the foyer was a pile of packs stacked by the door. Felix grabbed a small one from the top and opened it up.

"It's right here," he said, holding up her bag.

"Oh," she said, surprised. "I didn't put it there."

"The maids must have packed it," he said lightly. "I heard them grumbling about how you should be doing your own packing."

"Oh," Emya blushed.

"Oh no, don't feel bad. They were kidding. Someone should have told you they were going to pack for you though."

He patted her on the back reassuringly. "Breakfast is in the kitchen, go eat if you're ready." He ambled back up the stairs, buttoning the rest of his shirt as he went.

A bit sheepishly, she took his advice and made her way to the kitchen. Perhaps she had overreacted a little, but if something happened to the Companion, she and Felix would both be in peril. Their magical connection to the object would cause them to pass out if they strayed more than a certain distance from it. It might even kill them.

Smells of savory meats and fresh bread filled the kitchen. Artyem was already seated alone at the table as the cook bustled around setting out food. Emya sat across from him and helped herself to the nearest plates of bacon, eggs, and nutty brown bread. Felix joined them shortly, fully dressed, and eager to be off.

"How are you feeling?" Artyem asked Felix with an appraising once over.

"Strong enough to make this journey, and eager to be home."

It hadn't struck Emya that Felix was going home. How long had it been since he'd been captured by the Kings? She couldn't imagine being homesick for the village, maybe that was why she hadn't considered he might be eager to go home.

"I know you are, but that's no excuse for pushing yourself when you're still not fully recovered," Artyem said.

"All the more reason. Our healers will be able to help me. Those here have done all they can."

"You could still stay behind and rest. I can return for you after I deliver the girls."

"Sorry, can't be done," Felix said cheekily. He waved towards the ballroom. "Did you not see that sendoff they gave us? I can't scorn their gesture by staying now, can I?"

"I can't believe you," Artyem said with a scathing look.

After breakfast, gathering their packs, and saying goodbye to the maids who wished them all a safe journey, Emya, Felix and Arteym stood outside in the growing dawn light. Evris and her family appeared in the dim light, striding up the road. Dressed for traveling and carrying a pack much larger than Emya's, Evris greeted them with the exuberance of someone who had slept well indeed.

Mr. Kabris exchanged a few words with Artyem, who assured Evris's father that he would do his utmost to ensure a safe journey and promised to send word of their arrival. Felix accepted hugs from her younger siblings and mother, who then embraced Emya.

"Be safe," Mrs. Kabris whispered in Emya's ear.

"Take care of yourself. If you need anything all you have to do is write."

She then embraced her daughter in a fierce hug and bid her the same wishes. Evris rolled her eyes, obviously, she'd experienced this several times already. Emya stood, a little dazed, half happy beyond measure for the motherly gesture, half missing her own mother acutely.

Hefting their packs, they set off through the silent, sleeping village, the Kabris family accompanying them to where the cobbled stone became a worn dirt path. They hugged Evris and Emya one more time and stood watching as the four set off on their own down a wide dirt path the mountains looming before them.

"Which one are we going to climb?" Emya asked Felix beside her. Evris flanked Emya while Artyem led them, though he needn't have; the path stretched out before them.

"The highest peak, there," he pointed. "As we get close, you'll be able to see that it is split into three peaks. Between those is Civim."

"It's suspended magically right?" Evris chimed in.

"Yes, or with magic reinforcement at least."

"What's it like?" Evris asked wistfully. "I mean, what's it *really* like? I've heard stories, but..."

"It's not very different from any other society except that the people who live there come from all over and have many different cultures and ways of life. It can be difficult to understand one another. You have to be patient. We all work together though."

"But it must be different with everyone doing magic," Evris said.

"In a way, but I don't think it makes our society different. Magic or no, people are people."

As the morning drew on Evris filled the time with ever-changing, easy topics for Emya to discuss. Felix regularly chimed in. Artyem kept silent, his watchful gaze moving across the land and occasionally come to rest in short glances toward Felix. Emya knew he was keeping a careful watch on Felix's strength, just as she was.

After a few hours, as the sun was just getting warm in the sky, Artyem called a halt. They sat beneath the shade of a large oak tree. A few hours more, Artyem stopped them for lunch. At their next stop, Felix became agitated.

"Another stop?" Felix said. His tone was polite, but it held a hint of contempt as Artyem guided them to a particularly shady outcropping of rocks. Emya wasn't especially fatigued but dropped onto the dirt and stretched out her legs. She was used to running around the entire day doing Kamala's endless list of chores and found Artyem's frequent rests a welcome change.

"I don't mind," she said as Felix stood reluctantly before them, his arms crossed. "I never used to take many breaks."

This softened him, as she'd hoped it would, and he lowered himself, sitting cross-legged in the shade. Evris looked between them, a crease in her brow, but said nothing.

Emya had seen how tired he looked each time before Artyem called for a rest and how each rest seemed to rejuvenate him. Evris didn't seem to notice anything amiss, so maybe she and Artyem were being a little too paranoid. Then again, Evris hadn't seen Felix when he was sick.

As the sun began to drop in the sky, Emya cast her eyes up toward their destination. She saw the tallest mountain split into three distinguished peeks. Artyem estimated they would arrive before nightfall. The afternoon's journey passed serenely. Artyem didn't make them stop again which pacified Felix. They walked next to a shallow creek for a while. Emya admired the tiny sparkling gold and orange fish darting around the water and burrowing in the silt.

The sun was setting as they closed the distance to the base of the mountain and the grassy plane gave way to a dense forest. As they passed the first few trees Emya was relieved to discover the wild and untamed difference from the Sanguine forest. Brush covered the ground, pushed up against lichen and moss-covered trunks. Vines climbed and snaked through the canopy. Though, as they proceeded, Emya felt a subtle change in the air. It became a little cooler, more unforgiving.

"We've passed the barrier," Artyem informed them.

"The what?" Emya asked, perplexed.

"Oh, I forgot that you wouldn't know," Evris said. "There's a barrier that protects my village from evil magic. It's been around our land since before it was settled."

Felix nodded. "Many knowledgeable mages from Civim have studied it for centuries and we still don't entirely understand its nature or where it came from. We've never seen anything else like it."

"I thought magic wasn't good or evil," Emya said. "It's a tool, isn't it?"

"Ah, yes. It doesn't keep all magic out, otherwise, how could we get through? What the village has considered 'evil magic' since their founding is what we now call raw magic, an uncontrollable, unbound force that occurs when you perform any magic. It's not inherently evil, but it can be very destructive and dangerous."

"I've never heard of that," Evris said. "Does that mean I let raw magic into the barrier when I did magic?"

"Yes," Felix said. "But only a little. And one property of the barrier that makes it so baffling is that it seems to absorb raw magic. Some things do, we know, but we have no idea how."

"Is raw magic what caused the mayhem in my village?" Emya asked quietly.

"Some of it. The Kings performed magic crudely. I don't doubt that it resulted in a fair amount of raw magic."

"What happened in your village?" Evris cut in.

"She doesn't like to talk about it," Artyem interjected. "And now is not the time either. You should save questions of magic until we've reached the security of the Citadel."

With little daylight left, they did not journey far into the forest. The terrain was beginning to slope upwards, and it was clear that Artyem wanted them fresh for the trek up the mountain at daybreak. Finding a comfortable spot underneath a large beech tree, they set up camp for the night. Artyem skillfully built a fire and Emya sat with Evris and warmed up listening to the two men discuss the journey ahead. It would take two days to summit the mountain, according to Artyem, though Felix fretted that it would take longer if they kept stopping. He sounded irritable and tired, nevertheless, he helped Artyem heat up some of the bread and cheese. Along with dried meats and fruit they had an enjoyable dinner though it was nothing compared to the meals provided by the Mellia's cook.

They took out the sturdy travel blankets and settled down to sleep. Emya was next to Evris, while Felix was across the fire. Emya couldn't help remembering the last time she'd slept across a campfire from him. That night she'd wondered if he'd be alive in the morning. Artyem sat in the shadows cast by the fire, keeping watch. The plan was that he would wake Felix halfway through the night, though she had a feeling he would let Felix rest a little longer.

As promised, the trek up the mountain the next morning was steep. The path was thick with roots and slippery with shale. Every member of the party except for Artyem was gasping before long. The path wasn't always clear, as the mountain terrain was left disheveled by landslides and rain.

While they walked, Evris alternated between chattering with Felix about relations between her village and the Citadel, and asking Artyem questions about himself, the Tritium Guard, and how he knew the path so well. During one of these moments when she was occupied with Artyem, Emya fell behind with Felix, as they were navigating a particularly dense patch of vegetation.

"You're doing well," she noted as they climbed over a fallen pine. Felix gripped her hand tightly as he helped her over, though Emya knew it was as much for his balance as hers. "I'm glad I didn't believe you when you said it was too late to save you."

"As am I. I owe you my thanks and my life."

Blood rushed to Emya's cheeks, not from embarrassment but shame.

"I don't feel like I deserve thanks. I didn't want to believe you. I wanted to be accepted by the Kings."

He smiled sadly, though it looked like he was trying to hide it.

"I know. You were their perfect victim. I would have tried to talk to you much sooner, but I knew how fragile you were. The Kings saved you from a terrible life. I believed if I approached you too soon, before you had an inkling of what they had planned, that you would reject me. Then you would tell the Kings that I was trying to pit you against them, and I would never get a chance to convince you again- until it was too late."

They walked in silence while Emya considered that, the only sound besides their footsteps was Evris and Artyem's low conversation. After a while, Emya noticed Felix watching her intently. His brow was creased as if something was on his mind.

"You still don't know if they were lying or not," he said gently. "You're wondering if it will be any better in Civim."

"Yes," she said. "I'm afraid I've traded one enemy for another."

Felix nodded. He looked disappointed but resigned.

"I don't think there is any more I can say to convince you," he said. "You'll have to decide on your own."

Whatever the outcome, going back to the Kings was unthinkable. Emya could have stayed with Mrs. Mellia, but that wouldn't stop Felix from using her in the same way the Kings had if he wanted to. No, she had to believe he wouldn't. After suffering so dreadfully how could he turn around and torment the one who'd helped free him? It was the rest of the mages in the Citadel that she couldn't be sure of though. There was little she could do once she was in-

Emya nearly bumped into Artyem, who had stopped abruptly, scanning the brush.

"What is it, Artyem?" Felix asked, voice low.

"Something's stalking us," he murmured. Evris shuffled back to stand beside Emya and took her hand.

"Is it a Faolgal?" Evris whispered.

"No," Artyem said. "It's a beast of the ground." He drew a large, serrated blade. "Get behind Felix and me."

Felix drew his blade, pushing Emya behind him. From the shadows of the trees, the creature slunk out. Its body was slim and feline, while its head resembled that of a snake with fur, dripping fangs bared menacingly. A rope-like tail swished from side to side. It emitted a hissing growl from between its fangs.

"A Darram," Felix murmured. The creature leaped. Artyem lunged, blade swinging. Emya closed her eyes, gripping Evris. A noise of distress startled Emya, followed by hissing and yelping that could only have come from the creature. With a sickening squelch, its cry went silent. Artyem crouched before the creature.

"Darram are solitary hunters, and there is no sign of another," he said, returning to them and sliding the blade back in its sheath. Felix sheathed his own.

"Does that happen often?" Evris asked, getting a good look at the slain creature before running to catch up to the departing company.

"No," Artyem said. "But I fear we may face more attacks before we reach Civim."

Evris shot a look of fear and confusion at Emya. Emya shrugged, not inviting questions she could not answer. Scanning the area quickly, Artyem motioned them to move on.

The terrain became increasingly difficult to manage. Around noon Artyem stopped them to rest beneath a steep, rocky slope.

"After lunch, we'll tackle this stretch," he said, handing out provisions. "Best to be rested. We won't be able to stop until we pass it."

"It doesn't take very long," Felix said before biting into a sandwich of bread and dried meat.

"I know," Artyem said too politely, as though he was trying not to snap at Felix. "But if anyone slips it could take a lot longer."

No one spoke. By now even Evris seemed to be aware of the tension between the two men. Artyem was an expert in the terrain and spent most of his time ensuring that Evris and Emya were able to safely navigate it, a job which sometimes took longer than any extra rest taken for Felix's sake. Felix was becoming more impatient and irritable by the hour. Lethargic, visibly drained, and unsteady on his feet, he did not argue anymore when they rested, though his desire to reach Civim as soon as possible had not changed. The longer the journey took, the more his irritability strained the journey. His frustrations ultimately manifested in a short temper with Artyem. Emya was glad that he had enough energy in him to put up a fight.

"So, Evris will proceed first, followed by myself," Artyem looked to Evris. "I will guide you and, if need be, I can catch you without falling myself. Then Felix will follow me and Emya will come last. Felix, you will guide her with your lead."

"Emya should follow you, as you know the way better than I," Felix said shortly. "I can go last."

"If she falls, she will knock you down with her. We'd be running the risk of injuring both of you."

"I could catch her," Felix insisted, anger flaring in his voice. To Emya's surprise, Artyem smiled genuinely.

"Like you did the last time we made this trip together?" he said.

Felix opened his mouth, then closed it, conceding. "Fair point."

"Back then you could do magic."

"Yes, I know."

"But you didn't."

"Alright, alright, enough," Felix snapped but his anger had dissolved into laughter. They ate lunch in a much lighter mood. Evris was enthusiastic about climbing up the slope, confident they would traverse it without incident. Emya agreed with more confidence than she felt, but she didn't want Evris to lose spirit. Yet she couldn't help the nerves it induced every time she looked at the imposing path.

They finished eating and rested a little longer, then they secured their packs and prepared to hike. They had only traveled a short distance before Emya knew it was going to be more difficult than even she'd imagined. The tiny, jagged stones slipped under their feet, and they had to lean forward at an uncomfortable angle to maintain balance. A quarter of the way up, Evris nearly slipped while trying to find footing on a root that Artyem had directed her to.

Emya was glad to be last. Following Felix's footing was easy, as he had very little trouble following Artyem. He took her by the hand when they came to the places Evris had difficulty navigating. Evris seemed to be thoroughly enjoying Artyem's attention, his careful directions, his helping hand on her back.

At one point, when they were about halfway to the crest, Evris slipped but Artyem caught her. They all froze as Artyem steadied himself. And with his arms wrapped tightly around her and his attention on the terrain, Evris shot a heady grin over his shoulder at Emya. Emya smiled and rolled her eyes.

As they neared the summit, the slope, which had appeared to rise at a constant angle from the bottom, now curved up at an almost impassable angle.

"I don't think I can climb this," Evris said.

"Here." Artyem leaned over her and stuck his blade into the stone and dirt just above her foot, and a second blade above that. Felix passed Evris his blade from around Artyem.

"Stick it there," Artyem indicated a spot a little higher than she was likely able to reach with her foot.

Evris stabbed Felix's blade into the dirt above then grabbed onto the hilt and pulled herself up, stepping gingerly onto the first blade beneath her. Artyem held his arms out ready to catch her, though Emya doubted even he could keep his footing if Evris fell on top of him. She pulled Felix's blade out and gripped a stone jutting out half an arm's length above her left shoulder.

As Evris swung the blade towards the point Artyem had indicated, the hilt she stood on slipped under her slightly, and she slid down. The blade in her hand pierced the ground just as she lost her footing. She clung to the knife as Artyem reset the blade below her and guided her foot back onto the hilt. With a little hop, Evris managed to lift her leg onto Felix's blade and scrambled onto the grassy, shallow slope above. She sat a little way up to wait for them.

Artyem and Felix followed with ease. Emya checked the first blade for security. It jiggled a little, but not so much that it wouldn't hold. Artyem and Felix crouched as close as they dared, talking her through it.

"Grab that rock to your right." Emya couldn't look up at Artyem to see where he was pointing, so she grabbed the rock that was nearest even though it was wide and hard to grasp.

"Now that rock above the next blade," instructed Artyem.

Emya grasped it but the rock dislodged from the pebbles.

"No, the one above it," Felix said.

With a slight frustrated noise, she grabbed onto the sturdier rock and hoisted herself onto the next hilt. The last blade looked as though it was falling out of the hole slightly, but it had held all three of her companions so far. She stepped onto it and outstretched her hand, reaching for Felix. The blade cut through the ground, slipping from under her foot. Emya fell, sliding down the slope then tumbling head over heels. Her right foot caught on a rock and twisted and wrenched around and slid on her back as the slope flattened out.

"Emya!" Felix called.

In a daze, Emya lifted her head to see Artyem slide sideways against the slope, an avalanche of pebbles rained down after him.

"Stay there!" Artyem shouted over his shoulder. "No, I've got her."

Artyem crouched at her side, quickly assessing her condition. Though she felt pain all over, nothing was as sharp and searing as what she felt in her ankle. She whimpered as Artyem's careful hands brushed her ankle. Pain shot up her leg.

He gently removed her boot. She gasped; a rushing roar filled her ears. Fighting through the fog that threatened to overcome her, she focused on keeping her eyes on Felix, who watched anxiously with Evris from the crest of the slope.

"It's definitely broken," Artyem said calmly.

Several remarks ranging from sarcastic to downright angry came to mind, but Emya was in too much pain to give them the delivery they required.

"I can set it temporarily. You'll have to see a healer as soon as we arrive."

"Alright," she said through gritted teeth.

Artyem took her hand, squeezing it with grim intensity. "It will be quick. Are you ready?"

"Just do it," she snapped. He nodded and with practiced precision he set the bone. Roaring darkness consumed her. When it passed, she found herself panting in the dirt. Artyem peered over her, concern etched deep in his features. Seeing she was lucid, he scooped her up.

"Arms around my neck," he said. Though her arms felt like jelly, she leaned against him loosely and gripped her hands together behind his neck. She rested her head against his shoulder and closed her eyes. With impossible skill and balance, he ascended the slope in moments. She opened her eyes just as he grabbed Felix's outstretched hand. Crouching down, Artyem gently dislodged Emya's arms from around his neck and laid her on the ground. Evris, kneeling at her side, took her hand and brushed Emya's hair aside.

"You're alright," she said, wiping the tears from Emya's cheeks. She hadn't realized she was crying, but now she felt the hot drops falling from her eyes.

"This complicates matters," Artyem said.

"It can't be helped now," Felix replied.

"It would not have happened if I'd been more careful," Artyem said.

"It would not have happened if I hadn't been rushing you," Felix countered.

"Maybe, but I'm eager to get home too. And I can't give in to those feelings. I must find safe passage to Civim for you three."

"You don't hold the entire burden. I know this mountain as well as you." Artyem raised his brow at Felix skeptically. "Well, almost as well. I am helping as best I can."

"You're useless without magic," Artyem said bluntly.

"Yes, I know. You keep reminding me of that."

"Let this serve as a wake-up call."

"Can we get back on topic?"

Artyem began to pace irritably, a little too close for Emya's comfort near the precipice of the steep slope.

"We're going to have to take turns carrying her," he said. "She cannot walk."

"I presumed," Felix said, his eyes following Artyem in a way that reminded Emya of the way he used to watch the Kings.

"I don't want to put too much strain on you either."

"I'll manage."

Artyem turned and gazed up the mountain, his brow creased in thought. The strain was evident on his features as he considered his extremely limited options.

"I can help too," Evris chimed in. Artyem looked at her as though he'd forgotten she was there before smiling appreciatively.

"Thank you for the offer, but I think we can manage," he replied.

That seemed to settle the matter, for which Emya was grateful. Artyem scooped her up and carried her a little way through the trees to where the terrain flattened out.

They set up camp for the night, though it was still early evening. Useless, Emya sat while Evris and Felix collected wood. Artyem busied himself setting up a perimeter of rocks around a dirt patch for the fire.

It was quiet. The only sounds were the scrape of the stones Artyem stacked and the conversation between Felix and Evris drifting on the cool mountain breeze.

If Artyem was mad at her or blamed her for the accident, Emya couldn't tell. He didn't trust her, she was certain of that. She didn't blame him if he resented her for hindering their trip. He'd been polite and helpful, but he knew about the Companion, her attachment to it, and precious little else about her. He had Felix's word to back up her story, which seemed to be enough for him to allow her to come along, but only a fool would have let his guard down when such a dangerous object as the companion held sway over her.

In the fading light, she could make out the dark circles under his eyes and the crease between his brows. Stress was evident in his features, and perhaps a headache on top of it all. A chill from the bite of the mountain air, shook her. She closed her eyes and pulled her cloak tightly around herself. A heaviness enveloped her.

"Thanks," she murmured, opening her eyes.

Artyem nodded arranging his cloak around her. She shifted to recline more comfortably against the tree, her ankle twinging with pain.

"I don't mean to be impatient," she said with a wince, "but are we almost there?"

Artyem sighed, "We're about halfway."

"Felix looks better," she said. "But I can tell he's tired, even if he won't admit it."

"He's worse than he looks." Seeing concern on her face, he explained. "He told you what happened to his magic?"

Emya nodded.

"As potent as his magic has always been, it would take a lot to drain it from him. I fear it will have lasting effects."

A chill shook her that had nothing to do with the dropping temperature.

"It doesn't help," he went on, "that he's connected to

a powerful and dangerous magical object."

This was the first time they'd spoken of the Companion since the night he'd interrogated her.

"Do you think his magic would return to normal if he was released from it?" she asked.

"I have no idea, though I imagine he would be recovering much quicker without it. He doesn't show it, but it's causing him a tremendous amount of anxiety."

Artyem was right about Felix hiding it well, but his anxiety did not surprise her. Whatever toll the Companion was taking on both of them, though as yet unknown, worried her immensely.

"You seem to know him very well," she said. "How long have you known each other?"

"All our lives," he said his tone lifting. This was clearly a more comfortable topic. "Did he tell you he was born to a guard family?"

"Yes," Emya replied. "He said he started learning magic when he was very young."

"He did not live in Civim until he was ten. We played together as children and visited each other until our paths naturally diverged. I had not seen him in months before he disappeared. And I did not believe I would see him again."

Artyem hung his head, arms resting on his knees.

"Is he different now?" Emya asked.

Artyem considered this for a few moments.

"Yes. Subtly. He's less carefree, though he never

really was. There is a darkness about him, sometimes, and I fear—" he stopped abruptly when Evris and Felix emerged from the trees, each of their arms burdened with enough wood to get them through the night. Artyem set to the task of coaxing the fuel into flame while Evris and Felix prepared their meal. Half an hour later, Emya accepted a toasted sandwich of cheese and meat from Evris, who dropped cross-legged beside her.

"How are you feeling?" Evris said.

"My ankle hurts a lot, but not so much when I'm distracted."

"Then I must distract you. While we were collecting branches I almost tripped into a large hole, but Felix saved me." She waved her hand across the fire where Felix sat, talking in a low voice to Artyem.

"Oh no," Emya replied. "Be more careful. I don't think Artyem's sanity would survive both of us being injured."

Evris laughed.

"I wouldn't have been hurt. It was just very noble of him to save me." She placed the back of her hand against her head in a dramatic gesture and then giggled. Emya laughed, but it turned into a wince when she accidentally twitched her foot. Evris combed her fingers through Emya's hair comfortingly.

"Oh, I wish you hadn't gotten hurt. Better that it had been me."

"So that Artyem would have to carry you the rest of

the way?"

Evris winked and giggled.

"Listen to me. Mother would be scolding me for my cheek," she changed the subject. "What do you think Civim will be like?"

"You would know better than I. I've only just heard of it. You grew up knowing about it."

"True," she said. "All the more reason I'm curious what you think. You have a different perspective."

"Well," Emya said. She pushed aside her fears and tried to recall the images that had come to mind whenever she'd thought about it. She imagined it wouldn't be like her village, nor would it be like learning from the Kings. "Felix says they will teach magic differently than my old teachers. I hope he's right."

"You've already had teachers?" Evris said, gaping at her. She looked impressed and maybe a little jealous. "You can do magic already?"

"A little," said Emya.

"Can you show me?"

Emya squirmed uncomfortably, then winced as she moved her foot slightly. "I'd rather not."

"Of course," Evris said, her voice gentle and understanding. "You can't do magic when you're in such pain. You might hurt yourself even more."

Emya gave a small, grateful smile, though that was not the reason that came to mind. She hadn't done magic since they'd left the Kings behind, and the connection to the object scared her. She didn't want to do any more magic until she was guided by someone who understood her circumstances. The feeling of having her power sucked away by the object still burned in the back of her mind.

"But what was it like to learn?" Evris persisted.

"It was difficult. Felix says they were not very good teachers, but they taught me a few things like how to keep a fire burning magically and how to levitate objects—"

"And break spells," Felix cut in. He dropped down at Emya's side, travel blankets in his hand. "She broke a spell over me and didn't even know it."

"You never told me that," Emya said.

"I only just remembered," he said, taking Artyem's cloak off her and replacing it with the considerably less warm travel blanket. Emya immediately resented losing the cloak, but it was getting colder and Artyem would need it while he kept watch. "I could not have transported us unless you had completely severed the hold they had over me."

"I didn't do that," she mumbled. "At least, I didn't do it on purpose. How do you know it was me?"

Felix shrugged. "Who else could it have been?"

"Amazing." Evris leaned back and looked up at the sky wistfully. "I can't wait to start learning."

Artyem tossed a blanket over Evris; she grunted in surprise.

25

"You'll have to wait even longer if you don't get your rest," he said and walked around to sit next to Felix.

"Want me to take first watch?" Felix asked. Artyem sighed.

"I don't want you to take any watch," he replied.

"Don't be ridiculous." Exasperation coated Felix's words though his tone was still genial. "You need your rest now more than ever."

"Alright, I'll take first watch though."

Felix helped Emya lay down, tucking her pack under her head as a pillow.

"Comfortable?" he asked.

"Enough." Her leg throbbed. She tried not to think about the cozy, soft bed at the Mellia's house.

Felix lay on his side and pulled his cloak and blanket up over his head. Evris curled up close, comfortingly warm. Emya lay awake long after Evris's and Felix's breathing became the even, inaudible breath of slumber. Pain throbbed in her leg. She couldn't get comfortable and moving too much caused the pain in her ankle to shoot up her leg, further banishing sleep.

The night sang with the song of hearty cool weather insects and the crackling of the fire. Artyem's still figure was silhouetted in the firelight. Emya wished Felix were keeping watch so she could discuss the Companion. Though it was secured in her pack, it loomed constantly in her mind. She wanted Felix to reassure her that their arrival at Civim would bring about a swift solution, though she suspected and feared it would not. After a while, she drifted into a restless sleep.

Chapter Two

It wasn't her aching back or her throbbing leg that woke Emya as the pale rays of dawn slipped through the trees, though they were the next immediate thing she was aware of. What roused her was the steady downpour of rain battering the little camp. She sat up blearily, careful not to jostle her leg. Felix and Evris were hastily rolling up their blankets and packing them away. Artyem appeared beside her.

"Nothing but a downpour wakes you, huh?" he teased.

"Afraid so."

He carefully took the blanket off her and began rolling it up. Felix, looking miffed with his pack slung over one shoulder, took her bag from behind her and slung it on his back. Crouching, he put one arm around her shoulders.

"This is going to hurt," he said. She nodded and put her arms around his neck. Her leg gave a hearty twinge as he slid his arm under her knees. She held him tightly as he hefted her off the ground. Pain shot up her leg. Artyem covered her with her cloak.

"We're going to take a longer route," Artyem informed them. "But it will be easier."

Felix made a low huffing sound that only Emya could hear from her proximity to his chest. Then he nodded.

Their boots scraping and squelching in the rocky mud, the group set off. Felix's grip was strong and his step was sure, but Emya wondered why Artyem hadn't tried harder to persuade Felix to let him carry her. It had been arranged before she woke, that much was evident, but she expected more last-minute bickering. It must have been the rain that played peacekeeper.

Evris walked next to them for a while, keeping up light conversation by telling Emya stories about wanting to be a mage when she was little.

"I begged my parents to send me to Civim. I cried for a week when they finally told me I could not go unless I already could do magic. Then after that, I tried my hardest to do magic."

Felix's deep chuckle vibrated through his chest and warmed Emya's spirits a little.

"How did that go?" he asked.

"Not well. I sprained my wrist jumping over a large ditch. I thought I might fly. I did *not*."

Emya couldn't help but laugh. Felix chuckled too.

"When did you find out you could do magic, Emya?" Evris asked.

"I've known as long as I can remember," Emya said. She did not feel like describing how confused she was when she was treated differently than the other children. Nor did she care to explain why she was seldom allowed to leave the house and had to watch the other children play outside, or why her home welcomed few visitors, and everyone who came was reluctant to enter the house, never stayed long, and regarded Emya with fear and fury whenever she was caught sneaking into the room.

"I must have done magic when I was too young to remember though because I never did any that I can remember before I was seven."

"Maybe they were just guessing?" Evris suggested.

"Could your mother do magic?" Felix asked, a hint of caution in his voice.

"My parents always insisted they couldn't. I never saw them do magic, but they taught me how to hide it, so I suspected they could. I think everyone else did too."

"Well now you don't have to hide it," Evris said cheerfully.

"Yeah." Emya appreciated that Evris did not

treat her with pity or as though she was delicate. Her optimism and sincerity put Emya at ease, but she wondered if Evris would be able to keep it up if she knew the harrowing details of her life. Emya dreaded to think that the knowledge might drive her friend away.

"Evris," Artyem called over his shoulder. "I want to show you something."

Evris clambered up the ledge a few feet above them where Artyem walked. At first, Emya thought it might have been a ploy to let Felix concentrate without the loquacious girl distracting him, but as they emerged from the trees a magnificent view of the valley below stretched before them. Though the clouds and drizzle obscured much of the valley, Evris's village in miniature was visible, as was the Red Forest and beyond. Artyem pointed out parts of the valley from their vantage point as he walked. He didn't seem to notice Felix falling behind.

"I think showing villagers their land from this view is one of his favorite things," Felix said. "It's too bad it's raining."

"They must come up here more often than I thought," Emya said.

"Oh, more than just the new mages, yes, but not too many."

"What for?" she asked.

"Many reasons. I believe Artyem hired a man who is familiar with the mountain to go ahead of us to let the

31

Magisters know we're coming."

"Why?"

"So someone will come looking for us should something happen."

"But what if something happens to the messenger?"

"That is unlikely. As a messenger, he will be almost as familiar with these mountains as the Tritium guard."

They walked in silence for a bit. Felix said he needed to concentrate on a difficult slope.

"I've been wondering something," Emya said after the terrain evened out. She had not wanted to ask this in front of Evris, but the talk of her parents had reminded her.

"Yes?" replied Felix.

"Can blood be magic?"

His brow creased as he glanced down at her. Then he checked his footing as he wobbled a little on loose dirt. A shooting pain went from her foot to her back, but she hid her discomfort, wanting to know the answer.

"Yes and no," he said. "Are you asking if magic can be passed down through bloodlines? Or do you mean it in a more literal sense?"

"The council told me I could not go into my parents' house after they died because there was blood in there. They said because I had magic that the blood might be contaminated with magic. They said I might step in it and spread it through the village. I might infect my neighbors."

"Interesting," Felix said. "And what did they say when you had a cut?"

Emya shrugged. "They didn't think it could be passed if I was alive."

"And what does that tell you?"

Emya had thought about it. At the time she had convinced herself that there was a difference between bloodshed from a living person and a dead one because she had to, but she'd never really believed it.

"That they probably don't know what they're talking about."

Felix smiled and winked.

"At best, they're so engrossed in their fear and conspiracy that they believed anything that anyone thought up as long as it wasn't too inconvenient. For example, it would be difficult to make sure you, a free-willed human being, can't run around spreading blood all over the place every time you scrape your knee. Or maybe they were hiding something in the house."

"I felt they were hiding something," she said quietly. "I don't suppose I'll ever find out what it was."

"You may, though perhaps it is better not to know."

"I have another question," she said, lowering her voice to a whisper. "About the Companion."

"What is it?" he asked with a grimace.

"How will I be able to learn magic while I'm connected to it?"

"What do you mean?" he said, perplexed.

"What if something happens? What if I'm doing magic and it tries to take my magic again?"

Felix tilted his head in a surprised but impressed manner.

"That's a very insightful question. What makes you think that could happen?"

"It happened to you and now you can't do magic."

Felix pursed his lips.

"Yes, but that was after years of fighting the object, having my magic drained. I was tortured and made to starve. Not to mention that when we teleported, whatever magic the Kings still had from the last time they drained me stayed with them."

"But I have hardly any control over my magic," said Emya. "What if I lose control and it takes it? What if I accidentally make the object do something, or what if it makes me do something I couldn't normally?"

"Strange," he said. "I was also wondering that. The Kings controlled my power with the Companion, preventing me from performing any magic. Beyond that and using it to take my magic, they didn't know what the Companion could do.

"Connected as I was, I learned about it. I had a lot of time and not much else to do besides trying to find a way to break free. From what I could tell, it never gave the Kings true magic of their own. It gave them command of my magic and through *that* they controlled the object. Whenever my magic was almost regenerated, I could almost command the Companion despite the prevention they put on me. They always drained me before I could manage to use it to take back my power.

"Yet they never gave any sign that they knew what I was doing. Had they known, they would probably have drained me more frequently. I think all they knew was that their power was weakening.

"It only occurred to me after our escape that the object never recognized the authority of the Kings. It only recognized the power of the mage connected with it. Because they were able to command it with my magic, I've concluded that it didn't matter who had physical possession of that magic so long as it was connected to the object. So, to answer your question, I do believe it is possible that the object can act with your magic without your knowledge or permission, though I could be wrong. I will ask your teachers to watch you closely. I won't tell them why unless they need to know, but they will report anything out of the ordinary to me, just in case."

"All magic is out of the ordinary," said Emya.

Felix laughed.

"True."

The rain did not stop except for short interludes throughout the day. Felix refused when Artyem offered to carry Emya.

"You kept watch. I'll do the carrying," he said

shortly. Artyem grimaced but did not argue. Not long into their trek, with the slippery terrain slowing them considerably, Felix began to struggle. He kept adjusting Emya, sending pain up her leg with each jostle. He almost dropped her when he stepped in a puddle that was deeper than he realized, and eventually admitted defeat. He handed her over to Artyem's arms. Felix said it was for her comfort, but she caught him shaking out his arms when Artyem's back was to him.

The group rested every two hours. Eventually, Emya lost count of how many times she changed hands. They continued walking after dark to make up a little lost time. Eventually, they found a spot under a large, thickly canopied oak where the ground wasn't so wet.

The wood around them was soaked. The cold chilled them to the bone. Emya curled up against Evris, both shivering. The tremors sent spikes of pain up Emya's leg, but she could not stop them. Artyem gathered a few branches, set them in a shallow, rocky hole, then sat and eyed them dubiously.

"It's going to be impossible to get these to light as long as the rain and wind keep up," he said.

Felix said nothing. Though he seemed calm and composed, Emya could tell that his patience had run out and he was very close to shouting.

"Maybe I can help," Emya said. Artyem gave her a not unkind but skeptical look.

"How?" he asked.

"I have matches in my bag."

"I'm afraid those won't help us if we can't keep the fire lit."

"If the matches are lit, I can make them burn the wood. I'm pretty good at fire magic."

Artyem's brow shot up in surprise.

"It's true," Felix said with an approving nod. "I've seen her."

"Oh, yes, please let her. I want to see!" Evris said with yearning. She had longed to see magic, particularly from Emya.

Artyem tapped his hands on his knees as though debating with himself.

"Alright," he said at last. He helped her dig the little box out of her bag. "Try not to light me on fire."

"I won't," Emya said confidently and struck the match. It crackled and came alive with fire. Before she could summon her magic to keep it burning a gust of wind snuffed it out. She tried once more with no luck. Felix and Artyem crouched close to her, blocking the wind and dripping rain.

"One more time," Artyem said, cupping his hands over hers. She struck the match and the fire burned bright and strong, protected by its human barriers.

"Take it to the wood," she said and handed the match to Artyem. He carried it gingerly, his other hand cupped around the small flame. What Artyem did not know was that his efforts were not needed, for Emya was already keeping the match alight. She was concentrating too intently to explain this to him.

He placed the lit match beneath the carefully stacked branches and stepped away quickly. With a twist of her hands and a spark of her will that enticed the fire to burn she coaxed the fire into a small arc that spun from the head of the match onto the logs. With a rushing, crackling noise the fire engulfed the fuel in a roaring blaze. Evris and Artyem gasped in surprise. Even a small, impressed sound came from Felix.

"I'll admit," said Artyem, watching the fire with interest, "I was not expecting that."

"I said she was good," Felix said, grinning unabashedly at Emya. She blushed and looked away.

Evris hummed a little disconcerted sound.

"I thought it might be a little more obvious. Not to say it isn't amazing, but it was almost like it might have happened without magic, though I know it could not have."

Felix nodded. "Magic is often subtle."

"Someday I might be able to make fire form, but for now I'll settle for increasing the intensity if it keeps us warm tonight," Emya said.

"Oh, you'll learn how to do that before long," Artyem assured her, placing a few more hefty logs on the fire. Immediately they burst into flame as if they had been bone-dry. Emya furrowed her brow in confusion. The fire shouldn't have burned the soaking wood that well without the aid of her magic.

Everyone's mood improved considerably as the fire crackled merrily in the rain. Artyem draped wet cloaks over low branches, sheltering them from the drizzle. They wrapped their blankets, which mercifully had been kept dry in the bags, around themselves.

"These are made from a special cloth my ancestors invented a long time ago that repels water. It's the way the cloth is woven, look." Evris stretched the cloth taut before her. Emya leaned in a saw that it was woven in a tight, complicated pattern. "The fiber is also coated in wax for added protection."

Artyem was overly attentive to the fire, but no one complained. The heat was slowly drying them, and the rain had finally broken by the time they had eaten and were stretching out on the damp ground to sleep. Felix, having convinced Artyem to let him take first watch sat next to Emya, peering out into the woods.

"How's your ankle?" he asked in a low voice.

Evris's eyes were closed, close to sleep. Artyem was already snoring next to her. For protection, Emya knew, but she also knew Evris didn't mind in the least.

"It hurts," she said, "but I can manage."

"The healers can fix it almost instantly, you'll see."

"I'm looking forward to it."

She drifted off into restless slumber. The ache in her leg pulling her out of sleep not long after, and at some point, the rain had started up again.

She woke as dawn crept over the mountain. Wet and aching and already in a very bad mood. The morning's trek passed mostly in brooding silence. Even Evris plodded along, her head down against the rain, though she shot Emya a bracing smile whenever they caught each other's eye. The rain let up around midday, a small mercy. Later, when they stopped to make camp for the night it was nearly dry. The setting sun peeked through the clouds. Artyem did not need help lighting the fire.

Their spirits had lifted when they set out the next morning. Artyem had assured them that this was the final stretch and all were eager to put the arduous journey behind them. Their spirits lifted higher as the mountain's three peaks came into view. The wild, narrow path gave way to a wide, well-kept road. Before them, a tall, glossy white stone arch stretched between two peaks. The roar of a rushing river drowned out the sounds of the forest.

"That's the Leis River," Felix said. "It's fed by the melting ice in the summer and by mountain springs in the winter, though it still freezes over up here."

"It flows through our land," Evris said. "All the way to the great Lake Addise. We used to go there in the summer to swim and fish."

Artyem stopped suddenly, tensing against Emya. A figure appeared from behind a thicket of thorns, clad in dark, heavy clothes, face obscured beneath a hood, blocking their way. Two more similarly clad figures flanked the first. Artyem relaxed.

"What took you so long Tyem?" The figure lowered his hood, revealing a rugged older man with ruddy cheeks that matched his bright red hair.

"Had a few setbacks. Thanks for coming to meet us just as we're nearing the end of our strenuous journey," Artyem replied, his voice dripping with sarcasm.

"We only just discovered you were on your way," he said. "Next time send word."

Emya felt Artyem tense for a moment then relax. "I did."

"Ah well, he must be wandering these slopes. Lost probably. I'll send a search party."

"I think you'd better."

Emya thought it was odd that a man who was supposed to know the mountain well would get lost. Though perhaps he'd suffered a similar fate as she had somewhere along a different path and had no one to help him.

The three men, for the other two had removed their hoods, revealing younger versions of the redhead, fell in step with Emya's traveling party.

"Who is this?" the older man asked, gesturing to Emya.

"This is Emya," Artyem said. "She's coming to study magic, at Felix's invitation."

Emya thought that was a strange way of putting

it, though she had not considered that she needed an invitation at all.

"Ah. Nice to meet you Emya. I'm Zier. These are my little brothers." He gestured to the two men behind him. "You had an accident I see," he continued, noting Emya's wrapped foot and ankle.

"Three days ago," Artyem said. "It slowed us down a bit, but we could not have avoided the rain either way."

"No. Do you want me to carry her for the rest of the way?"

Emya tensed. She did not want to be carried by the unknown man, though it was obvious to her that he was one of the Tritium Guards like Artyem. Artyem must have felt her arms constrict around his neck and he shook his head. The gesture was as much to loosen her hold as to signal his denial.

"We're almost there and she's not heavy," Artyem said.

Zier turned to Felix shaking his hand. "Good to have you back."

"Thanks," Felix replied.

The reunited guards and Felix talked of events that had happened since Artyem left to pick up Evris. Emya, having no context, understood little of what was said. One part she found a little unsettling, though she didn't know why.

"Master Trevylin has been anticipating your return for quite some time," Zier said.

"Is that so? I shall have to thank him for his confidence in me," Felix said.

"He does have a good intuition for these things."

"Indeed. How long has he been anticipating me?"

"Since last month, I believe."

The road rose up to a ravine in which the river flowed. A large, natural bridge, polished by wind and rain, spanned the width of the ravine and passed through the white stone arch.

They passed under the arch and emerged onto a breathtaking sight. Before them the three peeks diverged, creating a vast pit that swallowed the river. Suspended above the pit, three tiers of enormous rings descended from largest to smallest. Each ring was made up of circular platforms about half the size of Emya's village that were connected by sturdy rope bridges. The top tier was comprised of nine platforms upon which towers stretched, almost to the mountain peaks. The middle tier had six platforms and squat buildings, the bottom had three platforms with few buildings and a vast amount of green.

Emya took it in hungrily. Civim was more magnificent than she imagined. The bridge gave way to a ledge on the edge of Civim. They walked single-file down the edge of the cliff to a rope bridge connected to one of the platforms. The rope bridge was taut and didn't so much as tremble under their steps as they crossed. When they stepped off they were in a large courtyard.

The first platform was abuzz with activity. Passers-by turned to look at them curiously. Both men and women were dressed in plain gray and blue tunics with silver belts. The men wore black trousers, while the women wore similarly colored dresses made from a soft, textured material. They were led across the courtyard to a squat, sturdy house. It was warm and bright inside, and Emya saw several men and women clad in the same white smocks worn by the healers in Evris's village.

Artyem carefully deposited Emya in one of the clean, soft beds that lined two walls. Felix took the chair on one side of her bed and Evris sat on the other. The healer, an older, stern-faced woman, stood with her arms crossed. She observed Emya as Artyem explained what happened.

"I've been saying it for years. We need a real road up the mountain. This forging nonsense is going to get someone killed," said the healer in a deep, rich voice as she shook her head.

"And I've told you," Artyem said in an agitated tone. "No."

The formidable woman glanced sideways at him. "Are you hurt?"

"No."

"Then get out."

"Afraid I can't Mistress Haven."

Pointedly turning her attention from Artyem and

onto her patients, the healer went about examining Emya's ankle with practiced efficiency.

"Well at least it's set properly," she said. Emya glanced at Artyem, who was stone-faced. He wasn't one to claim praise. She smiled her gratitude at him. He nodded.

The healer placed her hand gently on Emya's ankle. Though she barely touched her, Emya winced as pain shot up her leg.

"This is going to hurt," Mistress Haven warned. Evris grabbed Emya's hand and squeezed it just as a searing pain engulfed her whole leg. Every other sense failed her, but after a few moments it faded away. Her clenched jaw hurt and her hands shook as she released Evris and Felix's hands. She hadn't been aware of taking his hand but she released it quickly when she realized that the pain in her leg was gone entirely, as though it had never been.

"Feel better?" the healer asked, patting her ankle.

"Completely," Emya breathed.

"Good." She turned to Felix. "You, on the other hand, aren't going to be such a quick fix."

"I didn't think so," Felix said. Another healer appeared with a bundle in his arms. He held it out for him to take.

Felix reluctantly took the bundle and stood up.

"I have some things to take care of first," he said.

"It can wait," the healer said flatly.

His eyes flickered to Artyem who answered with a short nod. Felix marched through a door into another room.

"Thank you, Mistress Haven. I'll take them from here." At the healer's nod, Artyem motioned Emya and Evris to follow.

Swinging her legs off the bed, Emya carefully placed her newly healed foot on the floor. No pain shot through her, not even a twinge. It bore her weight and she stood up with no trouble. After three days of being carried, it felt fantastic to walk again, though she was a little unsteady at first. Evris wrapped her arm through Emya's. The healer watched them go. Emya glanced over her shoulder and caught her scrutinizing eye. Then she turned away, apparently satisfied.

~~*~*~*~*

Artyem guided Emya and Evris through the towering structures that were built so close together that it was almost impossible to walk side by side. Emya was used to this, as it wasn't vastly different from her village except for the smallness she felt next to these four and five-level structures. Evris, who lived in a village that was big and open, kept bumping into Emya and the other people they passed, though she was too enamored to notice.

Emya gazed around, impressed with it all. Everything

was made of polished stone in white, black, and gray. The sharp-cornered structures stretched into the sky and curved into spiral towers. Large panes of glittering glass windows adorned every level of the towers. Heavy wooden doors were carved with depictions of galloping horses and riders swinging swords. So lifelike were they that Emya thought it might be possible that they would move. As she passed one door, the fierce, carved faces followed her, but she knew it was a trick, as some of the portraits in the Mellia Mansion did so because of how they were painted, or so Mr. Mellia had explained. Many of the walls of Civim were carved too, though the patterns were random and intended to please, she assumed, rather than record the great deeds of past, as the carvings in the council chamber had been.

Mages clad in blue and grey nodded at Artyem as they passed. Their curious eyes glanced over Emya and Evris.

"They look like mages, don't they?" Evris whispered. "Not just their clothes, the way they walk and hold themselves. Don't you think?"

Emya thought everyone looked the same in that all of them were distinctly different from the people in her village and Evris's village. She didn't have any idea how a mage was supposed to walk. The Kings were her only reference point and none of the mages of the Citadel walked or held themselves with the same arrogance as the Kings had.

"I think we'll probably look like that before long," Emya said, thinking of her pack filled with dresses. It would be a shame if she wasn't allowed to wear them.

"You think? Artyem never said anything about a uniform and my father didn't give me much money to purchase one."

Emya hadn't thought of that. She'd never had any money. Everything was either given or lent to her. "I don't have any money either. I suppose we'll both have to wear what we brought."

They giggled a little too loudly, drawing a glance from Artyem.

"I will arrange your meetings with the Masters for later today," he said, turning and walking backward. "For now, you can rest, eat, and bathe in the guest house."

"Not in that order I hope," Evris said as she rubbed her grubby sleeve between her fingers. "I want a bath."

"You and me both," Artyem said with a smirk.

They emerged from the confines of the towers to an open square with a fountain spraying clear, sparkling water into a midnight pool. A younger mage sat on the grass surrounding the pool. He was talking, reading, writing, and even doing a little magic. Evris gasped in delight as one young girl coaxed up a tiny waterspout.

Artyem led them to the tallest tower at the other end of the courtyard. There, they entered a small foyer and then went down a hall and into a charming bedroom with wood floors and rose walls. Gossamer, the fabric that adorned most of Mrs. Mellia's windows, billowed gently. At first, Emya thought magic was moving the curtains, but then she discovered that the glass had been pushed out, letting the cool mountain breeze in.

"I never thought of opening windows," Emya said. Though the canvas windows of her village sometimes tore and exposed the house to the elements, they were quickly mended.

"Some in my village's can open," Evris said, "but most don't because they might break. I've never seen single panes of glass this big. I would be terrified of breaking them."

Artyem, who had disappeared as they were assessing the room, returned after a few moments burdened with a large pile of cloth. He placed it on one of the two beds and separated it into two piles.

"There's food prepared in the kitchen. It's down the hall and to the left. If you need anything hold this tightly in your hand." He opened his hand to show them a small, round stone that was made of the same material as buildings outside. Its polished midnight surface seemed to have depth behind it, and Emya swore she saw stars when she peered into it. "Someone will come to wherever you are."

Evris gasped with pleasure while Emya's stomach twisted in knots. Artyem dropped the stone into Evris's outstretched and eager hand. Emya fought back the almost overwhelming urge to smack it out of her hand.

She would talk to Felix.

Artyem excused himself and left the girls to themselves. Emya picked apart one pile of cloth piece by piece until she eventually found two long, thin cream-colored towels and matching washcloths. One mage outfit for each of them was also included in the pile.

"I guess we won't have to wear our own clothes after all," Evris said, grinning.

"Yeah," Emya agreed listlessly.

They bathed in deep pools across the hall from their room. The warm, floral-scented water soothed Emya's nerves and released the tension and aches accumulated after several nights of sleeping on hard, rocky ground.

They dried off and dressed in their new tunics and wandered over to the kitchen. There they found a large pot of rich stew simmering over glowing coals. Together they sat and ate at a small stone table. Evris chatted happily about every detail of what they had seen so far. Emya listened but could not keep her gaze from flickering to the stone that rested on the table by Evris's bowl.

"What's the matter?" Emya's gaze darted from the stone to Evris's now concerned expression.

"Nothing," Emya replied as lightly as she could.

"You look as though you're not very pleased to be here," she pressed. "Are you regretting coming along?"

"No," Emya said truthfully. She had decided to give them more than a few hours to betray dark intent before she turned tail and ran, though the urge to do just that was growing. She still had the Companion if she needed it. "I'm just nervous about the interviews."

Though this was true enough, it felt like a lie.

"Oh." Evris gave a nervous chuckle. "Yes, I hadn't thought about that yet. Now that you say it though I'm nervous too."

"Some sleep will help," Emya said. Suddenly she was overcome with a long, deep yawn.

"Yes. Then we'll be nice and refreshed."

Together they brought their dishes to a water basin. Evris twisted a little silver handle, coaxing water out of a long, curved silver rod. She quickly washed their dishes while Emya gawked in amazement.

"How did you know how to do that?" Emya asked.

"We have an irrigation system like this in one of our greenhouses. It can be done without magic. You just have to use the natural flow of water, though I suppose this one has some magic too. I don't see where the water comes from."

Back in their room they fell into their soft, warm beds. Closing her eyes, Emya drifted into a deep slumber to the sound of chirping birds, leaves swishing in the breeze, and Evris's gentle breathing.

~~*~*~*~*

Emya woke with difficulty. Consciousness had

slipped into her sleep, wheedling its way through her subconscious, and gradually rousing every heavy, sluggish fiber. Slowly she became aware of the golden light permeating her eyelids. The sun was low in the sky. She sat up, now suddenly wide awake and afraid. She looked around and found Evris's bed empty. She jumped to her feet, her thoughts swirling. Why had she been left alone? How come no one had woken her? She wondered with fear if she'd somehow disrespected the Masters by missing their appointment. Casting around for the stone, she would use it as Artyem had suggested.

As if summoned by her tumbling thoughts, the sound of boots striking the floor preceded Artyem's appearance in her doorway. She whirled around. Her wild manner seemed to startle him, though he recovered his composure quickly.

"Are you alright?" he asked.

"Yes," she snapped. "Why does everyone keep asking me that?"

"Perhaps," he said slowly, "because you are not alright."

She began to shake all over, tears welling up despite her efforts to keep them at bay. Artyem, his brow creased with concern, took three long strides over to her and pressed her onto the rumpled blankets of her bed. He sat across from her on Evris's bed.

"What's the matter?" he asked gently.

"I've...I've," she began to sob. "I've missed my

appointment...with the Masters. They must be displeased with me... they won't let me learn magic. Why did you let me s...sleep so long?"

"You haven't missed your meeting with the Masters."

Emya rubbed the tears from her eyes and took a long, shuddering breath. "I haven't?"

"No. They are waiting for you whenever you are ready. Evris woke two hours ago. She tried to wake you but you could not be roused. We decided to let you sleep."

"Won't they be mad at me for oversleeping? I've..." she hiccupped, recalling incidents of Kamala waking her with a smack for sleeping past important village meetings. "I've disrespected them."

"You have not. You have had a long journey, they understand this. And," he added, carefully choosing his words, "they understand that you come from a difficult situation. They want you to take as much time as you need. If you wish to postpone the interview until tomorrow that can be arranged."

Something in her mind snapped into place and a sense of calm filled her. This was not her village. Making judgments was foolish until she knew these people better.

"No," she said, wiping away the last of her tears. "I'll see them today. I don't know what's come over me. I don't usually cry like this."

Artyem smiled kindly. "I know. I figured that

out the first time I met you. It's this place. There is so much magic concentrated here that it can overwhelm someone unused to it. Your emotions will be more pronounced than normal."

Images of unhinged villagers drunk on rampant magic superimposed on the narrow streets of the Citadel. She banished those thoughts.

"I'm ready," she said and wiped the rest of the tears from her face.

"Why don't you take a few minutes to refresh then I'll bring you to them?"

She nodded. He waited while she smoothed out her hair and splashed water on her face. She knew her nose was still red and that her eyes were puffy, but she didn't want to waste any time waiting for them to fade, especially since there was a chance she might start crying again.

With a deep, resigned breath she turned and followed Artyem out.

Chapter Three

Artyem walked beside her, his face set in a stern, almost threatening expression. The mage they passed pressed against the walls to clear a path instead of pushing past her as they had before. Laughter bubbled up inside her though she did not know why she found it funny. She was grateful that the onlookers didn't gawk at her.

She and Artyem crossed three bridges to get to a circular platform that contained a large semicircular courtyard. Towering above them was a large, ornate building with a façade of bluestone. Greystone pillars spanned the length of it. She was both impressed and terrified. Artyem must have sensed her apprehension and murmured, "Are you sure?"

"Yes," Emya said, swallowing and steeling herself against a tremble that she couldn't quite control. Together they approached a large door leading to an ornate hall.

"They're in here," he said.

"Wait," Emya said.

Artyem stopped, his hand paused over the door handle.

"Can you..." she began. "Will you stay?"

"If you wish."

"Yes, thank you."

With that, he opened the door. The room was small. A large, bluestone table took up most of the space. Two women and three men sat around the table, each one looking at Emya as she and Artyem entered. Emya looked at each of their aged and pleasant faces in turn. They regarded her kindly and showed no signs of impatience at being kept waiting.

"Welcome Emya," said the man in the center of the group, his wrinkled features warm and friendly.

"Emya, this is Master Kyn," Artyem indicated the one who'd greeted her.

"Mistress Tunin." He gestured to a small, wispy-haired woman without any wrinkles.

"Mistress Hanna." The woman next to Mistress Tunin was a dark, stately lady who looked as though she normally had a stern expression.

"Master Noah." A powerfully built man with curly

blond hair and a thick beard. His eyes crinkled in mirth.

"And Master Trevylin." The man who'd been mentioned by the guard Zier was tall and white-haired. He wore a long, well-maintained beard. He seemed to be trying his hardest not to appear imposing or stern, but these efforts did not quite reach his eyes.

They greeted her with nods and words of welcome in turn.

"Have a seat," Master Kyn said and indicated the only free chair. Artyem pulled it out for her and then pushed it under her as she sat down. Then stood behind her as Master Trevylin eyed him disapprovingly but did not order Artyem to leave.

"We're so glad to have you here," Master Kyn began. "Artyem has told us your story and we are incredibly grateful for the bravery and kindness you showed to Felix. If it weren't for you, he would not be here."

Master Trevylin crossed his arms and looked down, making it difficult for her to see his expression.

He seemed to be expecting a reply. Emya nodded. The urge to say that she had only wanted to save herself was difficult to resist. It wasn't entirely true, but she didn't feel brave or kind for doing what she did. Still, they didn't need to know that.

"Do you have any questions for us?" Master Kyn asked.

Emya thought about the question she was saving for Felix. She didn't know if they knew about the

Companion yet. Even if they did, she wasn't sure she would get an honest answer from them. Felix might not give her one either, but at least he would understand why she asked. She shook her head.

"We are aware of your unique situation with Felix. We will have to take it into careful consideration during your training, though we do not yet know in what ways it might affect you."

Emya nodded. So they did know.

"Your teachers will be watching you closely, though they have been instructed not to change the lessons unless they appear to affect you," said Mistress Hanna. Her voice was deep and stern.

Emya nodded again, feeling as though she should say something rather than bobbing her head like a bird.

"I think you already knew all of this," Kyn said. "You're anxious, I'm sure, to find out what sort of test will be administered to determine your abilities and acumen."

"Yes," Emya said, her voice no more than a soft squeak.

"Artyem tells us you already have some training, though it sounds rudimentary at best. He says you can control fire," Kyn said.

Emya glanced at Artyem. He nodded encouragingly.

"Yes," she said. Then she confidently added, "I can make objects float in the air too."

"Good," Kyn said. The others nodded approvingly.

"If you would oblige us, we'd like to begin. There are several ancient tests designed to assess your abilities."

What followed was a different test from each of the Masters and Mistresses.

Master Kyn asked her to demonstrate her ability to levitate objects by lifting a small wooden stick off the table, which Emya did with ease. Mistress Tunin asked her to fuse a short candle wick into a small cylinder of wax. The Kings had demonstrated fusing objects, but she could not quite get it. Emya focused on the wax, directing her power to the wick which sank into the wax right to the center. Emya smiled at it, elated until Tuin plucked the wick out of the wax with ease. Emya's heart sank. The wick should have been stuck in the wax as if it was a normal candle, though Tuin smiled at her, apparently satisfied. Mistress Hanna handed her a knotted piece of rope and asked her to magically untangle it. Emya was unable to make it spring apart as Hanna had demonstrated, but Emya had loosened it so that it came apart easily when Mistress Hanna examined it. Master Noah simply took her hands in his large, calloused ones. She felt the energy inside her jump when they touched.

"Hm," he said with a half-smile.

The only test she failed to even partially accomplish was Master Trevylin's. He asked her to transport Master Kyn's stick from the table in front of her to somewhere else in the room. Though she concentrated her power and willed it as hard as she could, the stick remained stubbornly in place. Trevylin sat back with his arms crossed, his expression inscrutable.

Emya sat silent as the Masters murmured to each other. Finally, Kyn spoke again. "Thank you, my dear. I think we can all agree that you have indeed had some productive training." He glanced briefly at Trevylin, who inclined his head almost imperceptibly. "But I think you would benefit from starting in a novice class, as there may be some aspects of your education that are lacking. I would hate for you to miss those."

Kyn paused, waiting for a reply. He might have expected her to argue but she was not about to contest their decision.

"Alright," she said.

"It might please you to hear that you will be sharing your lessons with Miss Evris."

"Oh," Emya said, surprised but pleased indeed. "Good."

"That's all. Artyem will take you to dinner. It was very nice to meet you."

Emya stood up as the other masters expressed their pleasure in meeting her and wished her a good night. Emya mumbled good night and followed Artyem out.

"That wasn't so bad was it?" he asked as the door closed behind them.

"No," Emya said. It hadn't been. "I'm not hungry though. Can we go see Felix?"

"I think Mistress Haven might not approve of a visit at this hour, but I will ask her."

He led her out of the State House into the chilly night. It wasn't very late but the moon was high in the sky, its soft light glittering off the stone path. Back to the first ring they went, to the healer's house where they'd left Felix.

Emya waited outside while Artyem disappeared. He emerged so quickly that she was certain that her visit request had been staunchly denied. Instead, he beckoned her in. Mistress Haven passed them in the little foyer on her way to a small office.

"Don't get him worked up. He's given me enough trouble already," she warned Artyem.

"You have my word," he promised. Emya followed him down a hallway and into a little, private room.

Felix sat up in bed, papers strewn about the blankets. He looked up and grinned when he saw her.

"How'd it go?" he asked eagerly.

"Fine," she said. "They said I get to be in lessons with Evris."

"Good," he said. "I was hoping they would. You'll excel quickly."

"As long as I don't have any problems with the Companion."

His smile faltered. "That's true. I'd like to say you won't, but I honestly don't know."

Emya glanced behind her, Artyem had gone. "Can I

ask you a question?"

"Of course," he said.

"When Evris and I were in the guest house, Artyem gave us a stone that we could use to call for help if we needed it."

Felix nodded. "Yes, it's an enchanted device with many uses. Most of the time it's used to send messages."

"I thought magical objects were dangerous," she said carefully.

"Ah," he replied, understanding quickly. "So naturally you assumed it was a sign of some nefarious plot on my part to convince you to come here so I could use you the way the Kings used me?" His tone was matter-of-fact and not unkind, but Emya had a hard time meeting his eyes. She stared at her hands in her lap, her face hot with a mix of fear and embarrassment. Maybe it had not been a good idea to confide in him. When he didn't continue with assurances that there was no plot and that she was being silly, she finally lifted her eyes to look at him. He was not gloating or amused; his features were etched with real concern.

"I never said all magical objects were bad. Simple ones like that stone are harmless, we understand the magic used to create them and they serve an important purpose. You'll see. As you learn, you'll understand that this magic business is very complicated, but I recommend not looking for signs of deception and evil in the magic itself. Get to know the mages that live here. Then I think you'll start to understand what kind of person uses magic for evil and what kind uses it for good."

"Couldn't you just tell me?" she mumbled.

"I could, but I think you'll believe me if you see for yourself first."

"I believe you," Emya said, though she wasn't sure that was entirely true. "I don't think you're going to take my magic with the Companion."

Felix's expression faltered in dismay for scarce a moment before he could hide it behind a smile.

"Good. I was worried," he said, half-laughing.

The sound of a throat clearing behind her alerted Emya to the presence of Mistress Haven, flanked by two other healers ladened with large baskets. Visiting time was up.

"It's time for your treatment, Felix," Mistress Haven said. "The longer you put it off the longer you will stay here."

Felix grimaced. "If I must."

The healers surrounded Felix's bed, unpacking their baskets, laying out towels and bowls with crushed herbs, and opening jars of sweet-smelling liquids.

Felix deliberately focused his gaze on Emya, ignoring the healers.

"We can talk more later," he said.

Emya left Felix to the care of Mistress Haven and found Artyem waiting outside on a bench not far away.

He was staring at a group of mages gathered down the way when she approached.

"Ready to go to dinner?" he asked. There was a note of impatience in his voice, though she suspected it was not directed at her.

Exhausted and a little queasy, she was not in the mood to eat. It must have shown on her face because Artyem wrapped her arm in his, supporting her. "Would you rather go to bed instead?"

"Yes."

Back to the guest house, they went as the sun dipped below the horizon and night set in. Lights glowed over the streets, not from candles or torches, but rather out of hanging lamps steady and bright. Artyem bid her good night at her room. She climbed into bed and closed her eyes.

~~*~*~*~*

Emya briefly woke when Evris arrived a few hours later and quietly got into bed. The next time she woke the sun was shining through the window and someone was gently tapping on the door. Emya rolled over and opened her eyes as a young woman slipped in.

"Good morning," the woman said. "I'm here to make sure you're ready to begin lessons today."

Emya sat up. Her head felt normal, free of the dizzying emotion from the previous day, but her stomach growled. Evris's eyes fluttered open in the next bed over. She sat upright immediately and looked around wildly. When she caught sight of Emya, she relaxed.

"I forgot where I was," she said breathlessly. "I've never been away from home before."

The mage handed them clean clothes and towels. They bathed again. Though Emya found it strange to have a bath two days in a row, it felt nice to be clean. Dressed and ready, they followed the mage out of the guest house.

"Where are we going?" Emya asked.

"The dining halls," the mage replied. "Where you ate dinner last night."

"Emya didn't eat dinner last night," Evris said. "I don't think she was feeling up to it."

The mage gave Emya a sympathetic look.

Emya felt a little guilty letting Evris eat alone last night, but as they entered the high-ceilinged hall filled with the smells of bacon and bread, she discovered that Evris had not been alone. Long wooden tables lined the hall. Seated at them were dozens of chattering mages. Evris led Emya to the long table at the front of the room. Upon it were dishes piled high with more kinds of food than Emya recognized. She filled her plate liberally with crisp bacon, sweet, nutty biscuits, fried eggs, and a chunk of strong but sweet tasting cheese. Then she fell into step beside Evris to find a table.

"Evris!"

A young woman, half-standing from her chair, waved at them. Waving back Evris wove through the tables and diners with Emya close at her heels. Four mages sat around the young woman who had called Evris, each smiling and greeting her while glancing at Emya curiously.

"Everyone, this is Emya, she's the one I was telling you about. Emya this is Runel." Evris indicated the one who called them. She was a pretty girl with honey hair, olive skin, and a heart-shaped face. "This is Rob," she continued and pointed to the freckled, lanky boy with red hair who smiled and gave a little wave. "Yiddol and his sister Urdith," Evris continued, gesturing to the almost identical blond siblings. They both gave her an almost identical smile. "And Lydia," she concluded.

Lydia was tall and strikingly beautiful. She seemed to be the oldest, and her long chestnut hair cascaded in gentle waves over her shoulders. Her full pink lips spread in a reserved smile as she acknowledged Emya.

Taking seats between Lydia and Runel, Evris and Emya began to eat. Evris kept up a lively conversation with the whole table while Emya listened, silent but attentive, minding Felix's words from the night before.

"And you're a friend of Felix's?" Lydia asked with a turn towards Emya. Emya tried unsuccessfully to figure out how the conversation had turned its direction to her.

"Yes," she said.

"How did you meet?" Lydia asked. Emya couldn't quite place her tone.

"Now Lydia," Runel said, "we've already been told they met on his travels."

"But perhaps Emya would like to tell us her story before she hears all about us. Or would you like us to go first?" she asked Emya directly. "You must be as curious about us as we are about you."

Emya wasn't particularly curious about them. She couldn't imagine there was anything about herself they would find interesting except for the Companion, and she couldn't tell them about it. Still, she didn't want to be an outcast, and they had no reason to treat her as one as long as she didn't give them one. It wouldn't hurt telling them a little.

"He came to my village," Emya said. "He discovered I had magic and he said I should come here to learn. My teachers in the village were not very good."

Murmurs of interest and amazement met this declaration.

"You've already had training in magic?" Lydia said with an unnatural amount of amazement. "That's unusual. We almost always find young mages or they find us before any other instructors."

"Where are you from?" Rob piped up.

"Uh." Emya actually didn't know where her village was relative to Civim.

"Her village is along Otillu," Evris said.

"The great plateau!" Yiddol said excitedly. "We're from a village near the base."

"That explains why we didn't find you before now," Runel said. "Very few people live up there, and even fewer mages are born."

"They are not all friendly to mages either," Rob said. "Or so I hear."

"What is the plateau like?" Runel asked quickly.

"Grassy," said Emya. "There are almost no trees for miles around my village."

Telling these politely attentive mages about her village turned out to be a good idea. When Emya left out the upsetting aspects of daily life, she found that there was quite a bit she liked about her home. Her listeners were especially interested in the big, shy cats that roamed the grassland and found the villagers' versatile use of the sturdy grass interesting and impressive, though Emya couldn't quite understand why. They used the resources they had. Was that so impressive?

The musical chiming of bells rang through the hall. This, explained Runel, signaled the end of the meal and the start of lessons. It was then that their guide from earlier appeared at their table.

"Hi Ojo," Runel said. Ojo greeted her in return and then turned to Emya and Evris.

"Ready?"

Evris promised to find the group at lunch and with that, she and Emya followed Ojo and the crowd of mages leaving the dining room.

So far, Emya had only been to three rings and on the same level. Ojo led them past the impressive, bluestone building where she'd met the master the night before.

"That is the State House where the Masters do their work and manage the Citadel," she explained.

Passing onto the fourth ring they filed down a long staircase to the ring below. Despite the upper rings covering the sky, the streets were still illuminated as though the sun was shining above them.

There was a significant age variation in the mages that pushed past them. Most appeared to be close in age to Emya and Evris, though the number of children was greater than she'd seen roaming the streets above. A sense of purpose emanated from the mages as they walked hurriedly into buildings, though they all chatted happily as they went.

Magic permeated the air. The hair on Emya's arms stood up as a mage, who was sitting on the steps of a large black stone fountain that gushed snow-white water, spouted sparks from her fingers. The friends who encircled her laughed as they watched gleefully. Emya glanced covertly at Evris and found her grinning excitedly. Whatever reservations she'd been harboring now seemed forgotten in the atmosphere of something new and unlike anything she had known before.

Ojo, Evris, and Emya then went up three steps and through wooden doors, delicately carved and gleaming with silver. They arrived in a large, brightly lit room. The floor, walls, and ceiling were all made of the same, polished stone as the rest of the citadel, though streaks of cream in white comprised the color. It seemed the stone could be found in any color. Chairs constructed out of red wood and upholstered with cream leather encircled the center of the room. In the center of the circle, with his arms folded into his sleeves, was a tall and imposing brute of a man. His stern gaze regarded them, as did the occupants of the chairs.

Emya recoiled instinctively. Except for his civilized clothing, this man had all the markings and features of the dangerous Kings. Evris, brow furrowed with concern, took Emya by the hand and gave the slightest of tugs.

"Master Nikola," Ojo said. "These are your new students. Evris and Emya." She indicated them in turn. Master Nikola nodded and gestured to two open chairs. Ojo left them without another word and Emya only made it to her seat thanks to the involuntary movement of her legs in response to Evris's tugging. There she sat with her arms crossed. Slightly hunched, she gazed around. The twelve other students were all on the younger side, though none could have been younger than thirteen. They held themselves with much esteem, sitting with straight backs and their hands in laps. Some had books open and almost all eyes were on the master, though a few shifted quickly in her direction.

"Welcome," Master Nikola said in a soft, deep voice. Though Azo rarely raised his voice above a calm, reasonable tone, there was always a hint of danger in his words. This man, though he reminded Emya of the King in his tone and appearance, had no trace of danger in his speech. "We worried your arrival would be much later, but the guard managed to get you here just in time for the start of this class."

He turned from them and addressed all of his pupils. "Magic has been taught for thousands of years, whether by a practiced mage or by oneself. There have been schools created for the select purpose of teaching magic specific to the region or whims of the founders. There have been schools designed to give students the most thorough education possible. The history of magic education is as old, intricate, and convoluted as the use of magic itself."

Titters of laughter met this pronouncement. Master Nikola went on, his features yielding the slightest satisfaction of making the class laugh.

"Today I want to impress upon you why Civim teaches the way we do and what you can expect to gain from learning our way."

One of the students, a smaller boy, raised his hand. The master nodded for him to speak.

"I didn't know there were other schools," he said. "I thought this was the only one."

Master Nikola nodded. "There are other schools,

particularly in remote parts of the world, where magic has not yet had the impact it has had in our lands and history. If you focus your studies on magic abroad, you might one day be sent to them as a student. However, I want to focus on schools of the past for now."

Emya's attention was soon rapt in Master Nikola's lesson. He spoke of the first organized schools millennia ago, discussing their purpose of producing and propagating magic in individuals rather than the mere accumulation of power. Schools were designed to produce more complex and powerful magic, even those designed to create magical armies. Woven into his narrative were aspects of mage history that she was already familiar with.

"This brings us to Civim," Master Nikola explained. "We are well past the point where we need to produce magic. Despite an effort to purge it from every individual in the world, you are all here. We know from our history that any attempt to create a mage army will result in a repeat of history, thus we see no reason to attempt it. Our neighbors might claim otherwise, concluding that a large gathering of mages in one place can be for no other reason but to form an army. We assure them that there are plenty of other reasons."

Nikola's words struck her then, though she did not understand it. Who in their right mind would want to form a mage army when they'd caused so much devastation? More importantly, why would anyone believe the mages of Civim were forming an army? Was it because they found any school of mages to be suspicious or did they have evidence?

"Despite its use and influence over the world for so long, we still do not fully understand magic. The purpose of this school, therefore, is to study and understand magic for better use. Though we have advanced our understanding to a point where it is possible we could improve the lives of the people of this land, attitudes towards magic are still too heavily influenced by past events. This limits our ability to make an impact on the world. Therefore, along with your studies in the use of magic, you must also learn and understand to what extent those abilities can be useful outside the Citadel."

The rest of the class pertained to neighboring countries, and Emya learned that the country they were presently in was called Aphira. She didn't know if her village was part of this country. Master Nikola explained each country's policy on the use of magic. Some areas were more lenient, while others were very stringent. She learned that there was one small, far away country called Didin that banned all magic and mages. She would never be allowed to go there as a mage, though she would never want to. To her surprise, some of her classmates seemed indignant at the idea that they were not allowed to enter an entire country.

"Since they have no magic to defend themselves, how could they ever stop us?" asked one boy.

"They have defenses," Master Nikola said, "There are ways to render the power of magic less potent or simply block it altogether. And I am endeavoring to impress upon you that it is better to respect the wishes of these countries than it is to blatantly defy them."

"I don't see why," the boy said.

"Why would you—" Emya stopped abruptly when she realized that the thought had passed her lips. Master Nikola turned to her, nodding encouragingly for her to go on.

Painfully conscious that the eyes of the class were on her, she finished. "Why would you want to go somewhere that doesn't want you there?"

"Why indeed." Master Nikola said softly, observing her with understanding. "There can only be a few purposes as far as we're concerned: causing trouble and dredging up old grudges and conflicts."

"What if someone is born with magic in a place like that?" asked a girl with her hand in the air. "Wouldn't a mage have to go there to get them?"

Nikola's face twitched as though he suddenly had a bad taste in his mouth.

"That's a complicated situation, though it does happen more often than you'd think. I will say we have contacts with those without magic who negotiate the safe removal of those individuals."

Emya squirmed anxiously in her seat at the words 'safe removal.' What would have happened to her if the

Kings hadn't shown up in her village? How many people were like her? How many waited for their own safe removal?

If Master Nikola noticed her discomfort, he made no indication, yet the subject changed abruptly.

"Can anyone tell me the three laws of magic set forth by the Magisite?"

Several hands shot into the air, though Emya was relieved to see several faces as confused as she was. Master Nikola pointed at random.

"Harm no living creature using magic," a pupil said.

"Correct. This law was set forth during the conquering period when magic was even less understood. Over time, as magic was used more often in battle, it became apparent that the use of magic to harm or kill had consequences. Magic often lingered over battlefields, raw, destructive, uncontrollable. It ravaged the surrounding lands, poisoning crops and animals. Whole kingdoms crumbled. We must never use magic to intentionally harm. Another?"

"Magic is not to be used to gain an advantage over those without magic," another student recited.

"Yes," confirmed Master Nikola. "This code of morality was adopted to prevent situations such as the one we see in Didin. Using magic in this way leads to tyrannical mage kings, anger between neighbors, and eventually war and oppression. Another?"

"Magic must be used with reason, not emotion,"

said a third student.

"That is correct. Though emotion was the original means by which magic was extracted and harnessed, our current practice requires a thorough understanding of the different kinds of magic and the qualities that define them. Using those principles, we can combine different kinds of magic to create powerful and precise spells. Furthermore, the direct connection between magic and emotion eventually drove many of the early mages mad."

Murmurs reverberated around the circle at this. Emya's growing unease diminished a little. The Kings had taught her to use her emotion. They claimed it was the most powerful and effective way to harness magic. Already she was seeing significant differences between their teaching methods and Master Nikola. In addition, her new teacher did not give off the same sense of danger as the Kings. She did not feel as though she were a prey animal in his presence.

Nikola dismissed them soon after with the promise of a more in-depth discussion at their next lesson. Ojo was waiting for them on the steps outside. Emya walked beside Evris as Ojo led them through three rings to their next lesson.

"That was a lot to take in," Evris said, "and we haven't even started doing magic."

"A lot of what he said was different from what I'd been told," Emya said.

"Different better?"

Emya shrugged. "I think so. The Kings would never abide by those laws. If these mages will, then yes, it is better."

Emya's gaze shifted from Evris to Ojo in time to catch a surreptitious glance from their quiet guide.

Their next lessons were more in line with what Evris had been hoping for. They learned first how to recognize the magic power that coursed through them, then they learned how to summon it and bend it to their will. Emya was pleased to find she'd been taught this correctly and demonstrated her prowess with ease. Evris had more trouble. She was among a handful who hadn't managed to conjure their magic by lesson's end. Flustered and embarrassed, Evris nodded mutely as their teacher, Mistress Lo, insisted it would come in time. Evris nodded when she was told to practice when she was relaxing in bed before sleep.

"How did you first do it?" she asked Emya with a whine. Her usual effervescent optimism suppressed by her frustration. They ascended the stairs to the first level on their way to lunch.

"More or less the way the Mistress said to, though I'd been accidentally using magic for some time before that."

"Felix said I shouldn't compare myself to you since you've had training, but you make it look so easy—also you didn't even have good teachers before! I can only conclude that you have more natural talent than I."

Emya blushed. "I don't know about that. Felix says they were bad teachers because they taught me how to use magic in a crude and dangerous manner. I still learned the basics though. You will too."

Evris smiled with relief.

Inside the dining room, they filled their plates once more and Evris found her friends from breakfast, except for one.

"Where's Rob?" Evris asked as she plopped into the seat next to Runel. Emya sat between Lydia and Urdith.

"He usually skips lunch," Yiddol said. "He takes extra lessons in natural magic. He wants to be a farming mage."

"A farming mage?" Emya asked. Yiddol nodded.

"He's from a large farming community. He came here so he could learn agricultural magic."

"I can't wait to learn that," Evris said. "I could help out in the greenhouses!"

"What would you like to do Emya?" Lydia asked, her tone had no hint of maliciousness, but Runel shifted uneasily in her seat, her brow furrowed slightly.

"I don't know," Emya said. "I haven't thought about it."

"That's alright," Runel said. "Most people don't know what they want to specialize in."

After lunch, Emya and Evris had one more lesson, though the subject was not about magic. Instead, they learned about reading, writing, and numbers. They were in the same building but not in the same room, as Evris had already been thoroughly educated on these subjects. Emya, whose village had few books and texts, found herself in a room with students much younger than her, though not all. There was a man much older than her who explained in a heavy accent that, while he was proficient in reading and writing in his language, he had come to Civim to study in the language that Emya spoke.

After the lessons, Emya met Evris outside. They were free for the rest of the day and Evris was eager to explore. Ojo appeared again, and this time showed them to their new room in one of the towering buildings in the second ring. On the fourth floor, there was a common area that was connected to five small bedrooms. Two girls were assigned to each. In the common area, two younger girls sat in large, plush white chairs. Books were spread on the table before them. The girls did not look up as Ojo led Emya and Evris through the common room to one of the bedrooms.

"Your belongings have already been brought to your room. Civim attire has been placed in the wardrobe as well. You've been provided one outfit for every other day. Bring anything you need to be washed to the laundry room on the first floor. Baths are on the floor below this one. Anyone here should be able to help you if you have any questions. Your schedule will be the same as it was today for the rest of the year, though in the spring it could change. For now, if you have any problems, you can always ask me."

Ojo left Evris and Emya to settle into their new home. The room was outfitted with two small beds that had been made up neatly and pushed up against opposite walls. Evris sat on the edge of one, bouncing slightly. Emya pulled open the wardrobe. Inside a board split the space in two. A small E.K. was engraved on one side of the board. E.M. was on the other.

"How did they know my initials?" Emya wondered aloud. Evris appeared at her shoulder.

"What does the M stand for?"

"Messam."

Evris's brow shot up in surprise.

"Like Pike Messam?"

"Who?" asked Emya. She'd never heard this name before.

"Pike Messam was an ancient sorcerer. Very mysterious. He only participated in one great battle between the ancient mages and it's said that he fought with a power unmatched by any. No one knows what happened to him after that. It was rumored that he experimented with magic. He pushed the boundaries and created things so incompatible with this world they had to be locked away in magic containers to prevent them from causing irreversible destruction."

"I don't know if I'm related. I don't even know who

my grandparents are," Emya said with a shrug. "It's possible, I suppose."

"Some people are proud that they can trace their ancestry to the old sorcerers, but most people with old names don't know or care. I was just wondering," Evris said lightly as she looked through the tunics and trousers that hung in her wardrobe.

Squatting down to examine two pairs of shoes on a small shelf in her wardrobe, Emya absently stroked the sturdy material. The Kings might have heard a family called Messam lived in her village, though it was unlikely. The mages of Civim knew though. How did they find out? And did they know if she was related to Pike Messam?

"Come on," Evris said. "Let's take a walk."

Chapter Four

When wandering the citadel at their own pace, Emya and Evris discovered many things that they hadn't noticed while being hurried along by Artyem and Ojo. Each ring, they learned, contained a district. The ring they lived on was the housing district for the students. The first ring, the one that was connected to the Bridge of The Arch, as it was called, was the metropolis district. They were both eager to explore there, as they already knew it contained the hospital and dining hall. Across from the hospital was a large gym. When they peeked inside they discovered a group of mages at sword practice.

"If we're not allowed to harm anything with magic, I suppose it wouldn't hurt to know how to use a sword,"

Evris said as they walked to the next ring.

"Isn't that what the guard is for?" Emya added as two men dressed in the garb of the Tritium Guard sauntered past. She looked behind her to see them disappear into the gym. Turning back around she nearly bumped into a tall, lanky boy. He neatly sidestepped her with a grin.

"Missed you at lunch, Rob," Evris said.

"I was getting extra help with my specialty," he said. Emya had never seen him when standing. Being on his feet made him look different. He was taller than Felix and Artyem and looked a lot older than his youthful face suggested.

"We heard," Evris continued. "You're specializing in agriculture to help your family."

"Yes," he said, a little red flushed his cheeks. "I hope to travel to other lands to help when droughts and disease damage harvests. I've started helping grow crops here. It's good practice."

"Where do they grow crops?" Evris asked.

"On the third level." He pointed to the ground. "We don't need too much space since everything grows fast because the soil is always fertile."

"I'd love to see them," Evris said wistfully.

"You can go down there any time. Just don't mess with the plants or anything. The farmers can get pretty protective." Rob pointed his thumb over his shoulder. "If you keep going to the Garden ring you can see some of my work in the roses. I'll let you guess which is mine."

"Oh," cooed Evris. "Yes, that sounds perfect."

Waving over his shoulder, he headed off towards the dining hall. The girls continued on their stroll. Unlike the housing ring, most of the buildings on the first ring were stout, two-story structures. Something caught Evris's eye in the window of one and she stopped to peer in.

"It's a shop," she said excitedly. "Let's go in."

Inside, a woman sat at a desk, her hands busy knitting a fine yarn into a glistening swatch of fabric.

"Welcome," she said as they entered. "You're the new arrivals, aren't you?"

"Yes. I'm Evris from the village below. This is Emya. She's from the great plateau."

"Very happy to meet you both. I'm Mistress Gian." She waggled a finger at Emya. "I thought you might be from the plateau. I made a trip there not too long ago. My first. Lovely, kind people. They traded me some of their unique sheep's wool." She held up a bundle of course yarn that Emya was all-too-familiar with. The sight of it made her itchy.

"It's very nonreactive to magic, you see," explained Gian. "It's a quality only found in the sheep of those parts. I'll use it to make special garments for some of my colleagues for their experiments."

"I never knew our sheep were special," Emya said, thinking of the silly creatures who were always wandering off and trying to eat her hair. "They always seemed so simple and normal to me."

Mistress Gian chuckled. "They would if you're not used to magic. Everything in that land seems to be more resistant to magic. Interesting, is it not, having such different perspectives?"

Emya smiled and decided that she liked Mistress Gian. While they were chatting, Evris had wandered deeper into the shop, looking at all the knitted goods. She rubbed the edge of a blanket between her finger and thumb.

"What currency do you take?" Evris asked. Emya, having no money and therefore little interest in the items, further wondered why anyone would buy anything when everything they needed was already provided.

"I'll take any currency. I can always use it when I travel. Here in Civim we usually deal in our own currency. After you've been here some time, you'll be allowed to take certain jobs in exchange for payment."

"Why?" Emya asked. "They give us everything we need; shouldn't that be our payment?"

Gian smiled a wide, toothy grin and gave an affectionate chuckle. "I think you'll just have to discover that for yourself."

Emya resisted the urge to demand why everyone seemed to think she should figure everything out for herself, but she didn't want to disrespect Gian. She knew that if something was freely given it could be taken away if she caused trouble. Thanking the mistress, Evris led the way out of the shop and down the narrow street. Savory smells wafted out of some of the shops they passed. Emya caught glimpses of mages sitting at small tables, eating and chatting happily.

Still baffled by the concept of separate, paid dining, she and Evris crossed the bridge to the garden ring and every thought went from her mind the moment they passed through the wrought iron gates. A garden, magnificent beyond even Evris's village, spanned the entire platform. A path of shimmering gold dirt twisted through lush flower beds and expertly trimmed hedges. There was even a small forest of many different trees. She and Evris marveled speechlessly as they walked through the garden. A narrow brook wound its way around the garden. Aquatic grass and flowers swayed and bobbed in the gentle current. A white and gold stone bridged connected the paths over the brook. They peered over the stone balustrade and watched the brightly colored fish swim past.

The path wound through the forest to where several girls, young and older, were picnicking in the shade of a great oak. A bird chirped melodiously above. A scarlet flash passed over them. Emya ducked and Evris gasped.

"A Phoenix," she breathed. The scarlet and gold bird perched above them, pruning its feathers. A small, gold feather that had been plucked from its wing drifted lazily to Emya's feet. Evris picked it up and secured it behind Emya's ear.

"Phoenix feathers are good luck," she said, taking a step back to admire the effect. Self-conscious though she felt with the ornament in her hair, Emya left it to please Evris.

Beyond the trees was the rose garden, its fragrance drifted pleasantly through the forest. Emya inhaled deeply. Images of fruit and grass, salt and soap, honey and dust accompanied the myriad of smells.

A rainbow of colors flowed from the shrubs. There were climbing vines and bushes covered in more roses than they should have been able to bear. Some were red, white, pink, yellow, or a mix thereof. Others bright blue, gold, silver, dark purple, aqua. A patch of brightly-colored orange buds caught Emya's eye. A distinct smell of citrus emanated from them.

"I don't know why," she said to Evris, who crouched down to inhale deeply from a delicate bloom, "but I think these must be Rob's work."

Evris laughed. "I was thinking that too. Must be his hair, right?"

They giggled as they weaved their way through the roses and to another, less impressive flower bed. The sun was setting and the shadow of the peak cut through the dimming light.

"We should head to dinner now," Evris said. "But I want to come back here again soon."

Among the first to arrive for dinner, they had their

choice of empty tables.

"What an amazing day," Evris said between mouthfuls of potatoes. "I can't wait to try more magic tomorrow. I think I know what I was doing wrong. I know I can get it."

Emya agreed. "You will."

"I just have to practice."

Emya nodded, her attention much more focused on the roast duck she was cutting up. She'd never had duck before.

"My parents are probably cooking dinner now," Evris said, her voice cheerful but with a hint of longing. A quick assessing glance of her friend suggested that there was no homesickness behind Evris's smile.

"Singing and dancing around the kitchen," Emya said.

"I wonder if they miss me."

"Probably," Emya replied.

Evris's expression faltered into one of dismay for a moment.

"I mean, of course they do," Emya said quickly. "But I'm sure they're happy you're here just as much."

"Yes, of course," Evris laughed. "We haven't seen Felix or Artyem all day. I wonder if Felix is still in the hospital."

"I think so," Emya said. She intended to check on him before bed, but she hadn't told Evris that. Something inside her didn't want to share Felix with Evris.

"Artyem is probably outside the Citadel tending to his guard duties. I wish he could have said goodbye." Evris frowned into her plate. "I hoped he might come to lunch with us. Some of the other guards eat in here."

Evris waved vaguely at two Tritium Guards seated at a table in the corner. They were the same ones they'd seen going into the gym. Emya hadn't told Evris about the conversation she'd had with Artyem when he told her that he didn't like magic. She decided it was still best not to tell Evris.

"I don't think he likes it here," Emya said. "There are a lot of people and very little space. He seems to prefer solitude and open air."

"Yes," Evris said. "I think you're right. Maybe we can go visit him sometime, wherever he lives."

"Sure, but I don't know if we're allowed."

"Who should we ask for permission. Ojo?"

"Maybe. She might point us in the right direction."

The scraping of chairs, clinking of plates on wood, and the animated conversation of their dining group arriving interrupted Evris and Emya. Runel greeted them cheerfully.

"Hi Evris, Emya. How was your first day?" she asked.

Emya faded into the background as the conversation turned to their lessons, interests, and hobbies. Lydia invited Evris to join her someday in a sewing group. Emya was invited too, though mostly as an afterthought. Runel, however, thought this wasn't the best idea, as this kind of sewing required extensive knowledge of constructive magic.

Emya and Evris were both finished eating before their friends, so Emya gathered her dishes.

"Let's go," she whispered to Evris.

"Right now?"

Emya stood and took her dishes up to the table. Evris reluctantly followed.

"I want to see Felix," Emya said when they exited the hall. There was no reason, she decided, not to invite her, Emya knew that Evris would be hurt if she found out Emya had gone without inviting her. "Want to come?"

"Yes!" Evris brightened instantly, though it miffed Emya that Evris would have rather stayed with her new friends. It was silly to be jealous, but Emya was afraid of what would happen if Evris became too distracted by the new and interesting people of the Citadel.

Emya laughed inwardly at the irony. She'd lived most of her life without any real friends and it had never bothered her. Now she was terrified to be friendless once more.

Felix was seated at a table with papers spread out before him but still in his nightclothes. He smiled with relief when he saw Emya and Evris enter and tossed aside his pen.

"I've been so bored!" he said. "I've had no one to talk to."

Pulling up chairs, they told him about their day.

This time though, Emya spoke as often as Evris.

"Yes, the garden is magnificent," Felix agreed. "Did you see the bees?"

"No," they chorused.

"They're all different colors. It's a side effect of the magic used to protect them from the plants they pollinate. I see you met the phoenix." He lightly touched the feather tucked in Emya's hair. Though his hand barely brushed her, a tiny shiver ran down her back.

"How much longer are you going to be in here?" Emya asked.

"I don't know yet. Mistress Haven is growing tired of my asking," he said with a little sigh.

"Take as much time as you need," Evris said kindly. Emya frowned but did not speak. She was impatient for Felix to be fully recovered with his magic returned so they could work on the Companion.

"Thanks, but I do have pressing matters to attend to. They've already sent me a year's worth of work," he gestured to the papers spread before him. "And this is just what Mistress Haven will allow."

As if summoned, Mistress Haven appeared and ushered the girls out. Emya wondered just how high freeing them from the Companion was on his list of pressing matters. She hoped he would be able to convince his superiors that it was of the utmost importance.

"And you, go to sleep," they heard Mistress Haven

snap at Felix before the door shut behind her.

The common room was filled with girls around their age, though they didn't recognize any of them from their earlier lessons. Some of the girls introduced themselves, but Emya could feel her eyes drooping. Evris had no issue striking up a lively conversation. Emya slipped away to their bedroom and shut the door, silencing the noise beyond.

Reposed in the silence, she pulled off her tunic and hung it neatly in the wardrobe. She dressed in the soft nightgown from Mrs. Mellia and fell into bed.

She was not quite asleep when she heard Evris tiptoe in and dress for bed. The last thing she heard before nodding off was the rustle of sheets. Then, piercing her deep slumber, came a sound like thunder. Emya jumped out of bed. Danger, escape, the Kings—all of this snapped through her mind at once. She felt the need to run but the unknown rooted her to the spot. She caught sight of Evris sitting up in bed. It looked like she was trembling. A high-pitched scream pierced the air and spurred Emya to act. She stumbled to the door. Evris followed, latching onto her arm.

Emya cracked the door open and peered out. The common room was filled with smoke, stinging Emya's nose with the foulest stench. Girls milled about, their noses pinched between their fingers, calling out in anger and disgust.

"Oh," Evris said distastefully. "Stink bombs. Gross."

"What?" Emya asked.

"They just make a loud noise and a bad smell," Evris said before climbing back into bed. She muttered grumpily about being too tired to do magic in the morning. Closing the door, Emya sat at the foot of her bed and listened. The low voices and laughing of boys were pierced by high-pitched anger from the girls. Eventually, both were interrupted by the sharp, stern lecture of an adult, silencing the dispute.

Quiet settled once again, but between the lingering stench and fear of another attack, Emya's sleep was unrestful, drifting in and out.

As the sun rose, bathing the little room in light, she climbed out of bed and tiptoed into the deserted common room. The unpleasant odor still lingered. She hoped it would be gone by the end of the day, but she had no idea how long such things lasted.

The bathroom was empty, much to her relief. Stepping carefully into the shallow pool of warm water, she lay back and soaked her hair. The light, floral scent of the water washed away the odor.

Lathering her head with soap, she combed her hair with her fingers. After rinsing loose hairs from her fingers in the bath, she watched the dark strands dissolve in the enchanted water. Though she was slowly discovering the many ways magic was used all over the citadel, she was sure she lacked the experience to fully appreciate the exact delicacy it must have taken to enchant the water to constantly remain clean. Tempting though it was to float in the warm water all day, the sun had risen higher in the sky and soon the bath would be occupied by other girls starting their day.

Sure enough, as she dried and dressed the door swung open and three chattering girls strode in. Emya slipped past them into the halls that were already bustling with activity. The common room, no longer empty, sounded like a town meeting back in her village. There was much grumbling and talk about last night's commotion. Emya found Evris dressing in their room.

"I don't think I made any progress last night," she said wearily. At Emya's questioning look she added, "At summoning my magic."

"You will before you know it," Emya said encouragingly.

After a quick breakfast they hurried through the rings and down the stairs to Master Nikola's lesson. It wasn't quite as interesting as the day before. He spoke on the histories of countries that Emya had never heard of, and it was only at the end of the lecture that he explained what it had to do with magic. It was no wonder Artyem had known she'd been lying about what the Kings had been teaching her if he'd ever been subjected to a similarly thorough education.

She liked their next lesson much more. Mistress Lo was a no-nonsense teacher. She started the lesson by asking them to demonstrate magic, paying particular attention to the students who hadn't been able to summon their magic the previous day. By the middle of the lesson Emya was levitating multiple little stones at one time.

"Well done everyone," said Mistress Lo. Emya looked up from the stones she was twirling around just above the floor, while Evris watched with envy. "I think most of you have made sufficient progress with the basics."

Evris crossed her arms and sulked beside Emya. She still hadn't managed to show any magical ability, though Mistress Lo didn't seem too perturbed. She assured Evris again that it would come in time.

"Once you can summon your magic, the question becomes what to do with it? Early sorcerers spent a great deal more time experimenting and understanding magic than they did putting it to use. We benefit from their initial findings, but it would be a lie to say that we understand magic much better than they did. The nature of magic is still mysterious to us, in fact its very existence is an anomaly. It doesn't seem to be of this world, rather it may have been summoned here by mistake.

"Magic can be used in four ways," she continued before taking a small potted plant from the window and placing it on the floor in the center of the room.

"There is the natural form." She waved her hand over the top leaves which immediately began to bud and flower. "Which is used to affect the world around us. This is very similar to strength magic, which is used to affect humans and animals by making them stronger, or healing, or enhancing senses."

She put the plant back and borrowed a chair from one of the young boys. He stood, arms crossed, watching apprehensively as she placed the chair in the center of the room. Seeing his worry about having to stand for the rest of the lesson reminded Emya of how the Kings had once made her stand for several hours. They had meant to teach her something about magic. The lesson remained a mystery, but her legs hurt just thinking about it. She hoped Mistress Lo wasn't about to attempt the same lesson.

"Constructive magic is the term we give to magic used to manipulate the creations of man."

She touched the chair and it fell to pieces. The clatter caused the students to jump in surprise. After a graceful flourish of her hand, the piece sprang back together forming a table. With another flourish, it became a chair again.

"It is closely related to our last form, elemental magic, which is the manipulation of non-living things. Stone, minerals, water, fire, even wood, and bone can fall into this category. Life, it seems, gives a thing a particular quality to which magic behaves differently. We understand the difference between living, formerly living, and non-living things, however, we don't know why a formerly living thing takes on the same qualities as a thing that was never alive with respect to magic.

"Perhaps this is something for you to study if you're ever considering a specialty in magical research. Furthermore, when that quality is lost in death it cannot be returned by magic. A non-living thing cannot be given true life, nor can a dead thing be brought back to true life. Many sorcerers have repeatedly tried and failed to bend or break this principle, and many suffered unspeakable consequences. I will say no more on that subject until you are better equipped to understand the gravity of their actions."

She paused and looked at each pupil in turn as if challenging them to ask for more. Feelings of fear, confusion, and a little bit of longing must have been apparent on Emya's face because Mistress Lo's gaze lingered on her a moment longer than anyone else. Emya had never considered using magic to bring her parents back. She hadn't considered using magic for much at all until the Kings arrived. Even then, the idea of bringing her parents back by a means they'd find crude and disgusting had not crossed her mind.

When Emya realized that Mistress Lo was talking again she banished those thoughts and returned her full attention to the lesson.

"Elemental magic requires knowledge of the element to be manipulated. The better you understand what you are trying to manipulate, the more precise the magic," the Mistress explained.

Emya was beginning to realize that she understood very little about the world around her. Mistress Lo went on to describe the properties of water, dirt, and rock. The Kings had never taught Emya anything like it.

A soft noise of realization escaped her lips as Mistress Lo explained how fire burned. It was then that Emya understood exactly what she had to do in order to start a fire with magic. Evris shot her a questioning look.

"Tell you later," she whispered.

After the lesson they headed to lunch, joining a crowd going the same way. Evris chattered on about her frustration.

"Maybe I was wrong," she said. "Maybe I don't have any magic. How long until they realize they've made a mistake and send me back? Will you come to visit me in my shame?"

"There hasn't been a mistake," Emya said absently. A murmur oscillated through a group of kids that had caught her attention, though she couldn't quite figure out why. "You'll get it."

"You looked like you understood what Mistress Lo was talking about. Or did you just realize you forgot something at Mrs. Mellia's house?"

"No, I think I figured out how to make fire with magic. But I'll have to try it to find out."

This started Evris off on another self-deprecating

ramble, which Emya did not hear. She heard something in the crowd that sounded familiar. Many conversations were in languages and dialects she could not understand until the trill of a younger girl caught her attention.

"Emya. My sister told me about her. She's in the same dormitory. Doesn't talk to anyone other than that girl she came with. Avoids even looking at anyone."

"Oh dear. That's classic cast-off behavior," said a slightly older boy. "That's how Fiend Feriv was when she first came here. I hope she doesn't turn out like her."

"Me neither, but my sister says we should stay away from her. Just in case she--"

More students joined the crowd, pushing the kids further back so Emya couldn't hear the rest of the conversation. Rattled, she pushed through the crowd, anxious to get to the dining room. Evris followed in tow.

Emya sat at the table and picked at her food while Evris chatted with their friends. No, *Evris's* friends. The rest of the group didn't even try to talk to her now. Did they think there was something wrong with her too? Was everyone talking about her behind her back?

She had no way to know, but she was certain that she didn't want to end up like Fiend Feriv, whoever that was. Just because she was quiet and shy didn't make her some kind of fiend. This was something that she could control, and she vowed to make at least one friend besides Evris before the end of the week.

~~*~*~*~*

Several days passed with very little progress for Emya. Evris, in contrast, finally managed to summon her magic and nearly knocked Mistress Lo to the ground with a burst of power and enthusiasm. Emya enjoyed the time spent thereafter comparing what it was like to use magic. Emya had always felt it deep inside her, something to be pulled up like a buried memory. Evris compared it to finally putting to words a feeling she couldn't quite grasp before.

"I always knew it was there, you know, but it was always just out of my reach. Does that make sense?" Evris asked.

Emya agreed. She'd felt that way before, but it was not at all how she experienced magic.

"Magic must be different for everyone," Emya said. Evris nodded in agreement.

Encouraged by the easy, steady example of Evris's friendship, Emya tried to imitate her. Making friends was like a contest to Evris, one she always won. Emya watched her whenever she introduced herself to someone new. She treated everyone with the same enthusiasm. Every time she behaved as if each individual was the most interesting person she'd ever met. Try as she might, Emya couldn't emanate her blithe cheer and accepting nature.

Even so, Emya's attempts were increasingly

stymied as her fellow mages seemed to be distancing themselves from her. She noticed that they wouldn't meet her gaze, let alone stop for introductions as Emya had seen them do to Evris on several occasions. Along with the increase of unintelligible murmuring wherever she went, Emya felt even more convinced that a rumor was being spread about her.

She dragged her feet moodily behind Evris on their way to Mistress Lo's lesson. Tears welled up but she fought them back as she entered the classroom. She would not be caught crying by those who already thought she was sullen and volatile.

She had feared that her teachers would be like the Kings, but she had never imagined being treated as a dangerous pariah, as her village had treated her.

Anger flared through her, and the bowl of water in front of her fountained into a perfect stream into the empty bowl beside it.

"Excellent Emya," Mistress Lo said. "Can you tell me what property of water allowed you to make such a perfect arc?"

"Tension." Emya parroted the notion Mistress Lo had been teaching them, though she didn't understand it. Anger was the main property that had created the arc of water, though she knew she wasn't supposed to be letting her emotions fuel her power. Master Nikola had just spent his entire lesson lecturing them about the dangers of using emotion rather than understanding.

"Yes," said Mistress Lo. "Very good."

At least her magic skills were coming along nicely. She was usually the best in every class where there was magic demonstrated. Evris, though surpassing her socially and in master Nikola's lessons, needed extra help.

"I understand what she was saying about the tension of water," Evris said. "We use it to irrigate the greenhouses. But I can't for the life of me figure out how to--"

"Excuse me, Mistress Lo?" Felix stood before them looking strong and healthy. Emya hadn't realized his improved appearance on the journey up the mountain was still the cold shell of a man. Now his complexion glowed with color and warmth. His dark hair was thick and wavy, his lips full and red. Beside her, Evris exhaled a little too fiercely to be a sigh. "Can I have Emya for a moment?"

"Of course," said Lo.

With a nod from the mistress, Emya felt all eyes on her as she hurried past them and through the door Felix was holding open. As it gently swung shut behind them, Emya heard the whispers starting up again. If Felix noticed, he made no indication.

"How are your lessons going so far?" he asked lightly. She didn't answer immediately, not wanting to complain to him about her apparent inability to interact with the other students, though it weighed heavily on her.

"Fine," she said at length.

"What's wrong?" he asked, having read the distress in her expression.

"Nothing," she said, forcing her expression into something neutral. Felix didn't press the matter. He was still as careful around her at times as he'd been when he'd been enslaved by the Kings. Emya had been happy enough to ignore his pain. Not that she wished him any ill, and in her heart, she knew he wished no ill on her, but the doubt shared between them was natural. Nevertheless, their connection to the Companion compelled them to trust one another despite their doubts.

He stopped on the bridge they'd wandered onto in the direction of the housing ring.

"I don't want to keep you away from your studies for too long. I have been sent to ask you for the Companion. The masters want to examine it with me."

"Oh," she said, a little surprised. "Certainly. I don't have it on me though."

She realized then that it might not have been a good idea to leave the Companion unattended in her room where anyone could find it, but Felix did not scold her.

"Lead the way," he gestured. Together they made their way to the building where she lived.

"I used to live in the house next door," he said with

a gesture to the building where the boys lived. "We used to sneak over here to talk to the girls and play pranks."

He chuckled a little.

"Oh yes," Emya said with unhidden contempt. "I've discovered that very pleasant activity myself."

"What did they do?" he asked with scarcely suppressed mirth. Emya explained the events of her first night, grimacing at Felix's barely contained laughter.

"I'm sorry, I should have warned you," he said.

"It's alright," Emya sighed. "It was just unexpected."

"As a good prank should be, though I fear it was not the best first impression for you."

Emya shrugged. "They apologized after."

"Good."

She led him into the shared bedroom and then to the wardrobe. Nestled in her traveling cloak in a small drawer was the Companion, a dark secret in the peaceful light of the Citadel. It was a relief to hand it over to him.

"I'm surprised someone hadn't taken it before now," she said. "You told them about it as soon as we got here."

"They decided to wait until I was able to guide their examination before attempting to study it."

"But they could have taken it anyway," she said. "I'm sure they found it in my things."

Felix gave her a puzzled look. "They knew you had it. I don't see why you think they would search your things."

"Kamala used to go through my things when she

suspected I had stolen or was hiding something, which was quite often," Emya said. "She said it was her duty as a leader, though she never found anything. I guess I assumed they would do the same."

Felix smiled sadly. Emya did not like being pitied or thought a simpleton because she didn't know how other people would behave.

"Well, they might have," she added defiantly. "They took my stuff from the guest house to this tower. They had the opportunity."

"That's fair," he said. "Allow me to attempt to set you at ease. No one is going to invade your privacy or search your possessions. Not unless you give them a good reason."

"That's the part that I don't trust," Emya said. "What constitutes a good reason to them might not be what I expect."

"True," he said, turning to leave. "I hope you will let me know if anyone does something to upset or concern you."

"Who else is there for me to ask?" she said.

"If you find anyone else to confide in, I'll consider that a good sign."

Anger and frustration bubbled up inside her. She couldn't yet imagine trusting anyone enough to confide in them, especially when the whispers and rumors were pushing everyone away from her. She trusted Felix. She had to. Their fates were twisted together until Felix could unravel the secrets of the Companion.

Chapter Five

Felix walked her back to the class, promising to tell her when he learned anything new about the Companion.

"Come find me any time. I live in the eighth ring," he said.

Emya knew that the eighth ring of the first tier was private housing for the Masters, Mistresses, and others who worked in the Citadel. It was restricted and encircled by a tall wrought iron fence forged in the shape of climbing vines. Access for all others was limited to a path that linked the seventh and ninth rings.

"I'm mostly in the State House, working," he added.

"What do you work on when you're not trying to separate us from a dangerous magical object?"

Felix chuckled. "Before I was taken by the Kings I was experimenting with elemental magic."

"We're learning the basics of elemental magic," Emya said. "With water and fire."

"That's good. You need to understand how some of the basic elements of the world work before you can learn about natural, strength, and constructive magic. Beyond that, elemental magic becomes much more complicated. It's also the branch that contains transportation magic. You'll have a lot of fun when you start learning that."

They talked about the different types of magic until they returned to the classroom. Though they hadn't been gone long, Felix was so knowledgeable about Mistress Lo's lesson that Emya felt she hadn't missed anything.

Though the pleasant surprise of seeing Felix had improved her mood the whispers she heard on the way to lunch quickly cut into her good humor. This time they were so pronounced that even Evris noticed them.

"What in the world are they talking about?" she muttered to Emya. Two younger girls hurried by, shooting frightened looks at Emya as they passed.

"I don't know," Emya said. "They're afraid of me for some reason. I heard some talk about someone called Fiend Feriv. They're comparing me to her."

Evris hummed speculatively. "I've never heard of her, so probably not some notorious sorceress. We should ask Runel. I'll bet she'll know."

"I don't want to talk to them about it," Emya said flatly, looking down at her feet. She didn't want to admit to Evris that she suspected Evris's new friends of believing the rumors.

"Then ask Ojo," Evris said, without any indication that she thought Emya was being silly for not wanting to ask Runel or the others. "I bet she'll know."

"Alright. I'll ask her."

In the dining room, Emya scanned the tables in the hope to find Ojo, but she was absent. After lunch and her afternoon lessons, Emya resolved to seek her out.

That afternoon, while Evris was meeting with Runel and Rob to work on getting her magic up to par, Emya wandered off to find Ojo.

The narrow streets were crowded with mages. They chatted among themselves as they passed, but Emya could still feel the itch of backward glances from the younger mages. The older mages seemed to ignore her.

Disregarding their attention as much as she could, Emya wound her way through the housing ring towards the first ring. She'd seen Ojo going into the gym at about this time in the past, so she would check there first. Heading up a short flight of stairs and around a large, cylindrical hedge, she found herself in a narrow side street between two shops. Blocking her way were two younger girls and two boys. The boys weren't quite her age but they were older than the girls. Emya stopped short of them, leaving herself enough space to turn around and flee if she felt the need.

Emya half-turned when the bolder of the girls called out to her, "We just want to talk."

Emya turned back, her arms crossed. This was her chance to find out why everyone seemed to be afraid of her. Maybe she could assure them they had nothing to fear.

"About what?" Emya asked so softly that she doubted they could hear her.

"We wanted to warn you," said the girl. She was small with blond hair and naturally unpleasant features. She took a step toward Emya. "That you'd better not make trouble."

"I haven't done anything," Emya said, indignant. The two boys moved around the girls to flank Emya. She stepped back instinctively, but they moved with her.

"We know your kind," the other girl said. "You think the world owes you something."

The boys stepped closer; Emya could feel their body heat.

"No," Emya said, her tone pleading. "I don't."

"Hey," said a stern, low voice behind her. The four looked up, their faces guilty and scared. Emya glanced over her shoulder, reluctant to turn her back on the girls.

Artyem stalked up, towering over the boys. Arms crossed, he glared at each one in turn.

"Well?" he asked. "What are you doing?"

"Just talking," the blond girl muttered, red filling her cheeks.

"Talking?" Artyem said, his tone surprisingly pleasant. "It looks like you're surrounding her."

The boys pushed past Emya, into the girls, forcing them out of Emya's face.

"That's better. Now get going," Artyem said.

Turning away, the four hurried away. Emya sighed, relieved but dejected, as they rounded the corner and disappeared.

"Thanks," she said. Artyem nodded and shrugged.

"Those four have been causing trouble since the day I brought them here. And they weren't too well behaved on the journey either."

"You brought all four of them here at the same time?" she said, astonished.

"Was I that bad when I brought you two girls and a useless, still recovering mage?" he asked, mock indignant.

"No, not at all, but we behaved at least."

"True," he said. "No, I didn't bring them at the same time. I brought the girls together and the boys separately. They somehow managed to find each other when they got here."

He shook his head, and irritated pinch between his eyes. With a jut of his chin and a raised brow, he nodded her towards the shop next to them. Emya agreed with a smile and followed him into the little café.

The café was popular, Lydia had raved about it, and once inside Emya understood why. Beautiful crystalline tables filled the room, adorned with colorful flowers from the garden in bluestone vases.

Almost every table was occupied except for one by the window. An older lady was standing in the middle of the room serving delicate little pastries to a table of older mage girls. Artyem pulled out a blue marbled chair for Emya and took the one opposite.

"We're lucky there's a table," Emya said. It was a nice spot too.

"I know the Mistress," he said and jerked a thumb at the woman working her way over to them. "I messaged her ahead to save a table for me."

"You come here often then?"

Artyem shook his head. An emotion was playing on his face she could not quite decipher. "Only when I have business in the Citadel."

"Did you use the messenger stone to reserve a table?"

"Yes."

"I still don't understand what sort of magic that is."

"It's a complex enchantment but it's been perfected over time so that it can be learned easily when one has the skill."

"You know a lot about magic, don't you?"

"I've spent a lot of time with Felix and he often talks

112

about his work."

The Mistress appeared at their table and set two plates before them, along with two mugs of hot tea.

"I have other options," she said to Emya, "but he's going to insist you try this first. I'd just go with it if I were you."

"Thank you," Artyem said. "You are correct."

She hurried off to clear a table, already occupied by another couple.

"Have you had this yet?" he indicated the square of a layered pastry. Her mouth was full of the delightful texture of nuts, cake, cream, and the subtle sweetness of honey and cinnamon. She didn't answer right away.

"No," she said after swallowing. "I don't have any money."

It occurred to her just then that she could not pay for the pastry. Artyem must have seen it in her expression and smiled reassuringly.

"I know," he said. "This is my treat, but I imagined someone would have brought you here by now. New friends, or Felix, if he'd pull himself away from his work for five minutes."

"I haven't made any new friends," she said reluctantly. "I think they are afraid of me. They stare at me and whisper behind my back."

Artyem grimaced at his plate. "I'm sorry."

"Do you know about Fiend Feriv?" she asked. His head snapped up, his gaze tense.

"Who told you about her?"

"I overheard some younger mages comparing me to her."

Artyem let out a long, aggravated sigh before running his hand over his face. Emya's heart echoed the feeling.

"She was brought here a few years ago, not long after Felix disappeared. She came from Didin. Have you heard of it?"

"Master Nikola told us on our first day. They forbid magic there."

Artyem nodded. "Yes, and anyone born with magic is either concealed by their parents or exiled. Feriv was both. Her parents tried to keep her power hidden but one day she slipped. She was not much younger than you are now. When her neighbors caught her, they dragged her to the border and cast her out. We found her by chance. She had been wandering in the mountains, half-starved and delirious."

"So she was like me," Emya said. "Mistreated by her kinsmen."

"Yes and no," he said. "We didn't realize until too late what her true intentions were. She hated magic as much as anyone else in that country and despised herself for being tainted with it. She didn't want to be cast out of society or torn away from her family, but that was what she believed she deserved. When we told her about Civim, how they could help her learn magic

114

and that she could have a new home and a new life, she agreed to come. Enthusiastically. Half a year later she revealed her true intentions. She attempted to destroy the second ring while screaming about how we were dirty and needed to be cleansed from the world. I won't upset you with the details, but ever since there has been a certain amount of apprehension towards new arrivals, especially those who don't seem too excited to be here."

Emya laughed sarcastically. "And here I was worried about the same thing except I expected them," she flicked her hand up at Civim in general, "to want to rid the world of me."

"Your point of view is much more common than how Fervis saw things. I don't think we've ever found another that believes as she did. If such a person exists I doubt they would attempt an attack on Civim."

He took a long pull of his now cold tea. "You'll find troublemakers in any group, but I can tell you for certain that most of those looks you've been getting are not because they believe you're here to kill us all."

"Why then?" she said, her frustration no longer concealed.

"They're afraid to upset you. They don't want to give you the wrong impression of Civim. It could land them in a lot of trouble." He leaned forward and said in a low voice, "I'm not supposed to tell you, not until you've been here long enough, but there are very specific rules for how those who come from bad situations like yours are to be treated. We've had too many runaways found dead on the mountain."

Emya grimaced.

"I thought most would be happy to be in a place where they are accepted," she said.

"Most are. Some are less trusting, but I'm not talking about how your neighbors treated you. I'm talking about those Kings."

Emya cocked her head in confusion. Up until they betrayed her and she ran away with Felix and the Companion, she thought they had treated her fairly decently.

"Those such as the Kings who prey on young mages to enslave them and use their power, or in very rare cases, steal their power."

"You're saying that no one will talk to me because they're afraid that I might accuse them of trying to steal my magic?"

Artyem snorted a laugh. "Essentially. Or being held responsible if you run off and get hurt."

"Does everyone know about the Kings then?" she asked, dismayed at the thought. She was afraid of what they might think if they knew how she had turned a blind eye to Felix's suffering for her own selfish desires.

"No, not at all," he reassured her. "Most of the students here don't know the circumstances from which anyone else has come."

She sighed. "What should I do to put their fears at

ease?"

"Nothing. Do not worry, it will pass soon enough." He held up a finger sternly, "Just don't run off."

"I won't."

"Speaking of which, how are your lessons? Different from the Kings?"

"Yes," she said. "It's nice not having to guess what the teachers want me to do. The teachers here always tell me."

"That's a good teaching method in any endeavor. I had a teacher in archery who wouldn't tell me exactly what to do or what he expected. Put me off the whole subject."

"Do you mean to tell me that you're a bad archer?" she teased

"Yes, but don't tell anyone," he said with a wink.

The Mistress appeared beside the table to check on them, startling Emya.

"Want to try anything else?" she asked her kindly.

"No, thank you." Even if she wasn't so full, she wouldn't have presumed to take advantage of Artyem's kindness. Also refusing her offer, Artyem paid for the treat and suggested a walk through the gardens together.

"You don't need to get going?" Emya asked.

"I have attended to all my business for the day. I have only to check in at the Tritium Main Post later tonight."

Having no other plans before dinner, she accepted. She wondered if Artyem wanted to be seen with her as a way of sending a message to the other mages. Would seeing her on friendly terms with one of the guards put them at ease? Or would they interpret it to mean she was indeed a danger?

The true motivations for she and Artyem taking a pleasant stroll through the cool, fragrant night air, she could not divine. During their walk, Emya discovered that Artyem knew a great deal about the plants and the magic used to create some of the more breathtaking displays in the gardens. Though he said which mage had performed each work of magic and explained to her how they did it, Emya couldn't help but wonder if Artyem was jealous of the other mages. Though he claimed to mistrust magic, he seemed to have an appreciation for it. Clearly, he had no problem using magic items, such as the messenger stone. He certainly knew a great deal about magic and seemed to take pride in this knowledge.

"Artyem!"

They were in the rose garden when they heard the call. Turning, they saw Felix striding up to them.

"I didn't think you'd still be here," he clapped a hand on Artyem's shoulder with affection. "Then I got word that you'd been spotted in the garden and I had to see for myself."

"I was on my way out when I found Emya wandering

about on her own," he replied.

Felix cocked his head playfully.

"So naturally you had to stay and entertain her," Felix agreed.

"Of course, especially since you've been neglecting her. But now you're here and I can hand the duty over to you." He made to leave but Felix grabbed him by the arm and pulled him back.

"Not so fast. You never come to visit me. I'm not letting you get away so easily. Emya," he instructed, "don't let him get away."

"I don't think I could stop him if I wanted to," she said.

Felix, subdued on all sides, hung his head. "Very well, you can go, Artyem. It seems our busy schedules and your strong distaste for my company has brought our friendship to an end."

Artyem snorted, rolled his eyes, and smacked Felix not entirely playfully on the head.

"I didn't realize it would be so easy," said Artyem.

"You're cruel, you know that?"

"I have heard whispers of it, yes."

Together the three of them walked through the garden. Emya chuckling at their sardonic banter. It warmed her heart to see a side of Felix she had not yet known. A good sign of his recovery she thought.

"So, did you arrange this betrayal?" Felix said as they emerged from the garden and into the first ring.

119

He smiled mischievously. "Did you know he was coming and devise to keep him to yourself?"

"I didn't know he was here," Emya said. "Nor did I seek him out. He happened upon me, fortunately."

"Fortunately? Why is that?"

Between the two of them, Emya and Artyem explained to him the events of that afternoon. Felix frowned, his carefree mood reduced to the expression Emya was more familiar with from his days with the Kings, though not nearly as pained.

"I'm sorry," Felix said. "I've never heard of this Fiend Fervis."

"It happened while you were gone," Artem explained.

"It was never at the top of the list of topics to catch you up on."

"But you knew? Did you know they would think her another Fiend Fervis?"

"I thought it was possible that some might make the connection. I never dreamed they would confront her like that."

Felix sighed and shook his head. "I'm going to see to it the students never confront her again."

"No," Emya said quickly. "I can handle it."

"Emya," Felix looked into her eyes, his gaze heavy with tension and grief. "I will not have you living in fear and oppression as you did in your village. I promised it would be different here. I mean to keep that promise."

He turned to Artyem. "Let's take her to dinner. Then you and I are going to talk with Kyn."

As they walked through the Citadel, Felix smiled and greeted everyone as though nothing was amiss. Beside him, Emya could sense the tension. Or maybe, she was beginning to suspect, there was something about the connection between them that allowed her to sense what he was feeling. It was a different kind of feeling. With Evris, who she now spent a lot of time with, she could tell what she was feeling from her tone and expression. But with Felix, it was as though she could feel what he was feeling. She had no idea if the Companion might affect them in ways beyond their physical bond, but it was possible. She smiled to herself. Her thoughts were starting to sound like Felix. Perhaps that would help her become a good mage.

The dining room was nearly empty as dinner was just beginning. Felix found a table in a corner of the room.

"Is something else amiss?" he asked her as they sat. He was able to read her so easily.

"I'll tell you later," Emya said as she spotted Evris, Runel, and Lydia approaching. When they saw Felix, Runel and Lydia stopped short. Evris marched right up and set her plate down next to Artyem.

"Hi Felix," she said. "You look well."

"Thank you, so do you."

"I should hope so." Evris grinned and then shot a

confused look at Runel and Lydia. Both had approached with apprehension.

"Good evening, Master Felix. Is it alright if we sit with you?" Runel asked.

"Of course," Felix said with a careless wave.

Emya glanced at Evris, who shrugged. Runel and Lydia sat so straight and solemnly it was as though they were in the presence of a great and powerful ruler. Emya had never seen anyone treat Felix with so much respect. She supposed that it was technically true that Felix was a Master, though he didn't teach.

"It's not often we see you eating among us Master Felix," Lydia said, her usually haughty tone was now one of utmost civility. She sounded how Emya imagined one would speak to a king. The villagers never spoke to the Councilors like this, respectful though they were.

"I confess," he said, his eyes crinkled in mirth, "that I usually eat at my desk. My superiors don't believe I deserve any breaks after my unintended sabbatical. I work until I fall asleep. When I wake up I go right back to working. Though they chastise me even for those moments of rest."

He gave a long-suffering sigh.

"How tyrannical of them," Evris said, laughing. "I can't believe they get mad at you when you fall asleep at your desk."

"Yes, I suppose I deserve it. They tell me my snoring disturbs everyone else's work."

"They'll wish to send you on another sabbatical before long," Artyem murmured.

"You think?" Felix looked up wistfully. "Maybe a more pleasant one this time."

"Not if you annoy them so," Runel said, ever practical and the quickest, Emya noted, to weave herself into the threads of conversation. Though she looked as uncomfortable as Lydia, Runel seemed to keep her composure more easily as she ate. Then Emya noted that her utensil-free hand was clenched tightly in her lap.

"Perhaps they'll send you with me, Emya," he said with a wink. "I hear you're quite annoying yourself."

Emya gaped at him, wondering what possessed him to bring her into the conversation like that. Was he referring to the troubles she'd been having, or was he trying to send a message?

"I've heard the same, Master," Lydia said with a smirk. Emya's stomach twisted, suddenly unable to swallow the food in her mouth. She thought she might be sick.

"My younger brother reported to me that on her first day in Master Nikola's lesson that she bested him in a matter of Didin geopolitics with one question. He was not thrilled about that." Lydia shot a sly smile towards Emya. Felix burst out laughing.

"I heard about that. Well done Emya." Felix smiled at her, beaming with pride.

"I hardly call it well done," Emya muttered into her plate. "I don't know anything about other countries. I was asking an honest question."

"Yes," Runel said. "What you don't know is that you touched on the current political stance of most of the older mages, and that of Master Felix. They're all tired of fighting with the people of Didin, who will not be convinced of our good intentions."

"Didin exists because there will always be people in the world who don't trust magic," Lydia said. "They wish to live in peace without magic."

"I don't understand," Emya said. "What's wrong with that?"

"There are some among those who don't trust magic that believe violence is necessary to prevent the use of magic," Artyem explained. "That will always be unacceptable."

Emya's heart fluttered uncomfortably. She had lived most of her life with the exact kind of people who would do anything to prevent her from doing magic.

"Yes," Felix said. "And so there are mages who believe we should not leave Didin in peace because some there would hurt or kill us because of our magic."

"But fighting only leads to more fear," Artyem said. "And it reinforces their belief that magic must be met with violence. Most of the mages here understand that."

"Which is essentially what your question was addressing, and why my brother was embarrassed,"

Lydia said. She gave Felix the briefest of glances. "Our family has always supported peace with Didin. He did not mean to imply otherwise."

"I'm sure he didn't," Felix said diplomatically. "He's just a kid after all."

"I'm sure you were not so careless with your discourse when you were his age," Lydia said.

"I assure you I was, though it was not so widely publicized. Believe me, my superiors remind me of my more radical adolescence."

"Well I'm thoroughly lost," Evris said cheerfully. "Did anyone hear about the mess on the third level? I bet it was Rob's fault."

They all laughed, and the conversation turned to light gossip about the goings-on in the citadel. Emya, Felix, and Artyem finished eating before the rest.

"Emya, would you mind if I walked you to your room?" Felix asked as they stood up.

Emya could feel Lydia's gaze on her. "No, I wouldn't mind."

As she gathered her plate and cup, Emya caught Lydia glaring at her plate for a brief moment before turning a most gracious smile on Felix.

"It was good to see you up and about, Master Felix."

"Yes," Runel agreed. "We're glad you're back safely."

"Thanks," he said and gave them the same charming smile he seemed to have for everyone but Emya. Sure, he smiled at her, but it was different. Perhaps it was that the circumstance of their meeting was still too raw.

"Artyem, if you could go on ahead and let Master Kyn know that I'll be over shortly," Felix said as soon as they were outside. Artyem gave a curt nod and sauntered off.

Together, Emya and Felix headed towards the living quarters at a leisurely pace. Evidently, Felix was not in a hurry to speak to the other Masters, though he'd been upset enough before dinner. Maybe he'd reconsidered her request to allow her to handle it on her own?

"Well," he said. "What did you think about the conversation at dinner? Notice anything interesting?"

"I didn't expect Runel and Lydia to speak so formally to you. Should I call you 'Master Felix' too?"

He laughed, embarrassment apparent in his twilit features.

"I purposefully never introduced myself as such to you so that you wouldn't."

"When I first met you if you had told me to call you Master, I would have been very confused, as you were not even the master of yourself."

"Indeed," he said. "The Kings would not have allowed it for sure."

Emya tensed, she had not intended the conversation to go in this direction. Felix sensed her discomfort.

"Apologies. Let's not talk of them. Did you notice anything else besides their formality?"

"Yes, but I probably shouldn't say. It's speculation."

"Humor me."

"I noticed that Lydia made a point of explaining her views, as they align with yours. Is she worried that her family might be in danger if they think differently than you?"

Felix stopped and peered at her with a concerned look.

"Certainly not," he said not unkindly, "Though Didin is a point of contention among those who do not agree with the majority of the Citadel." His expression turned from concern to a mischievous grin. "Lydia has been pursuing me ever since her arrival. She's ambitious and sees me as the only one with talent and a position worthy of her ambition."

"That makes you sound like some kind of royalty."

He chuckled. "Don't spread this around, but I believe the Masters and Mistresses intend for me to take Master Kyn's place when the time comes. His is the highest position one can achieve here."

"Oh," Emya said. Shyness overcame her. "I didn't know you were so important."

He smiled sadly. "I'm not sure I want to be though. I have other plans, but I won't be able to accomplish them without help from the Masters, and I don't think they will approve them. My only choice is to do what they say or do nothing nearly as ambitious as I was hoping. I must rise above all of them and approve my own plans, hindered though I will be with the additional responsibility."

"Is there no other way but seeking the approval of the Masters?"

"Not really. But nothing is set in stone yet. I will tell them my preferred path when I'm ready and they may yet agree to it. I'm hopeful."

"I was wondering something else," she said.

"Yes?"

"I think I made a mistake. Should I have kept my mouth shut about Didin?"

"Not at all. We believe civil discourse is paramount for a peaceful civilization. That being said, there are controversial topics that could get you into trouble should you weigh in on them. Why do you think it was a mistake to speak of it?"

"I'm afraid that I don't think too highly of people who dislike magic. I was afraid, after what you said about those who would use violence against those who hate magic, that some might believe that I think the people of my village should be punished or something."

"Ah," he said. "I see."

"I don't want to punish them," she said firmly. "I only wish never to return to that place."

"I can assure you no one will believe you want to hurt anyone unless you say so."

Emya nodded. As usual, she felt both silly and relieved from expressing her concerns to Felix. She appreciated that he never mocked her. Though now she wondered if he chose his words so carefully because of the rules concerning how to treat her. Before long they arrived at the tower she called home. Felix opened the door for her. She snuck a quick look up at him as she passed. He had that smile he reserved for her, though it wasn't trained on her. Despite her attempt to be inconspicuous, he caught her looking.

"What?" he asked.

"I was wondering what you thought about Lydia's... ambition."

"Towards me?" he laughed. "I'm afraid her designs would be better directed elsewhere. Truth be told, she intimidates me."

The genuine laughter that overcame her surprised them both. "She would be very upset to hear that I think," she said through her laughter.

"I know, and I'm afraid of what she might do, as she is an exceedingly talented mage. So please don't tell her."

Emya wiped the tears of mirth away. "I won't. I don't know her well enough to talk to her about something like that."

Emya got her laughter under control as they arrived at the common room door.

"I don't want to risk flustering any of your housemates, so I'll leave you here," he said.

"Have a good night then," she said.

He half-turned away then rounded on her, swiftly scooping up her hand.

"One more thing," he said. His hand, warm and strong, squeezed hers. "I wanted to ask, what do you think of Civim? Besides this nasty business with some of the students, would you believe me now if I told you this is a good place and the people here have good intentions?"

Startled, Emya gazed into his earnest eyes, trying to formulate an answer. What she really wanted to think about was why it bothered her that Lydia was pursuing him. She thought she knew the answer, but she needed to think it over.

"Yes, I think I would," she said. "That is, I certainly don't see why they would harm me when I see no signs of anyone else being harmed."

"Well reasoned," he said. He lifted her hand and gently kissed it. Her chest fluttered with the erratic beat of her heart. His hand slipped out of hers. The sound of his retreating boots tapping on stone matched the pulsing in her ears. She turned and hurried into her room where she threw herself on the bed.

It was clear she liked Felix. It was impossible not to feel close to him, protective of him, after what they'd been through together. She was invested in his wellbeing, that was for sure, but she was coming to realize that he was kind, thoughtful, and did not patronize her. He tried to help her make a new life for herself, but he did not impose his idea of what that should be. She knew that he wanted her to be a mage, but he was going to let her figure out for herself what she should do. He didn't help her to make her think well of him either, it was just who he was. It was impossible not to admire him for his kindness.

She sighed. Jealousy towards Lydia was one thing. It was natural to feel that way, and it was a relief to discover that Felix did not reciprocate Lydia's feelings, but she did not know if that was because of another woman in Civim. She knew very little of his personal life.

With a sigh, she pushed herself off the bed and began to undress. Perhaps a night's rest would help her sort through her feelings. She was pulling back the blankets when Evris came in.

"Well," she said pointedly. "You're not going to believe what they said after you left."

"About me?" Emya asked softly.

"No. About Felix. I don't know what to make of it myself. They said he's some sort of prodigy. I mean, I knew he was smart, but they say he's going to be in charge around here someday, and probably soon. He's essentially a prince. And here I've been treating him like he's just another friend from the village. My parents would be shocked if they knew I hadn't been giving him due respect. Of course, neither have they, but that's not the point."

"He told me that himself, just now actually."

"That he's a prince?"

"No," she said with a laugh. "I don't think he'd ever

put it in those terms. But he told me he's going to take Master Kyn's place someday."

Evris sank onto her bed. She looked overwhelmed. "I can hardly believe the heir of Civim came to my house and had dinner. Wow."

"And your father threatened him too."

Evris clapped her hands over her cheeks. "He did! Oh dear!"

They burst into laughter.

"Apparently people think we're special since we arrived with him. They think he must have told us some secrets, or that we're exceptionally powerful. They think he was off looking for us. I told Runel and Lydia, who already know it was Artyem who was sent for me, that Felix wasn't sent for you. They wanted to know how he came to find you. I could not tell them that, as I don't know either. And I said if you'd rather keep it that way then that's your business."

"Thanks," Emya said. "I'd rather not talk about it."

As they lay drifting off into sleep, Emya's head churned. She wondered vaguely, in the last shreds of consciousness, what had transpired in Felix and Artyem's meeting with Master Kyn that night. Hopefully, she would have fewer whispers around her very soon.

Chapter Six

Sunshine roused Emya, drawing her into the waking world. The blankets wrapped around her were exceptionally warm and comfortable, and something inside her glowed with warmth and happiness. She couldn't remember the last time she felt so good.

As she and Evris dressed and prepared for the day, Evris chatted about Felix. It seemed the subject had not been exhausted the night before. Evris speculated about things Emya hadn't thought of and didn't care to. Who cared what anyone else thought of her friendship with Felix? Let them gossip about her gaining special favors from him. She was connected to him by a dangerous magical object that could kill them both. There wasn't much she could do about her proximity to him. Evris thought Emya needed to be careful, and considering what people already thought of her, Emya knew that Evris was probably right, but she didn't want to worry about that. Right then, Emya could think of nothing else except seeing him again.

She was distracted in all her lessons and didn't notice her teachers watching her carefully. She remained oblivious until Evris asked her what was wrong.

"Nothing," Emya said. "Just thinking."

"All the teachers are giving you funny looks. I think you're scaring them."

"I'm sorry. I'll be more attentive," she said.

Doing so was difficult. The feeling of Felix's soft lips lingered on her hand. She couldn't stop thinking of his smile, the one he saved just for her. As they walked to lunch, Emya was finally free to let her mind wander. Evris was deeply engaged in conversation with Rob, who seemed to run into them fairly often and didn't require much conversational input from Emya.

She was entertaining the pleasant memory of dancing with Felix during their last night in Evris's village when a familiar voice caught her attention. Felix was striding through the lunch-bound crowd. He came to a stop before them. Rob immediately ceased his conversation with Evris and stood straight and respectfully before Felix.

"Good afternoon, Master Felix," he said.

"Hi Rob, how are things going in the fields?"

"Just fine, sir, despite what you might have heard."

"I haven't heard any different. Keep up the good work."

"Yes. Thank you, Master."

Felix turned to the girls.

"Hi Evris, how are your lessons going? Are you still having a hard time with levitation?"

"Rob's been tutoring me so I'm getting much better," she said in her usual cheery manner. Whatever she thought about due respect she spoke as she always had. "What about you? Still causing trouble for your superiors?"

"Naturally. I'm sure they'll banish me from the Citadel before long."

"We can only hope, right?" she said with a wink. Rob shifted uncomfortably next to her. He appeared visibly startled at her casual declaration.

"Indeed," Felix said. "If you two could excuse me, I need to speak to Emya."

"Of course, Master Felix." Rob caught Evris by the arm and drew her away before she could protest. Evris locked eyes with Emya and shrugged.

"I still find it strange when they call you 'Master.'"

Felix blushed. "As do I, but I'm getting used to it. After all, it's what they were taught."

He motioned her to a bench under a shady tree near the edge of the ring. Sitting next to her, he gazed with the same intense expression he'd had back when he'd told her to run away from the Kings. Emya tensed, her warm feelings wilting as she braced for rejection.

"I haven't known how to tell you this. I meant to yesterday but I didn't want to trouble your sleep."

Emya waited, unable to speak. Seeing her tension, he went on quickly.

"It's nothing too serious," he said. "Just disappointing."

Emya exhaled slowly. "Alright."

"I haven't been able to increase the distance we can be separated. I was sure with Master Kyn and Master Trevylin's help that I'd be able to, but it seems it can't be done."

"Oh," Emya nearly laughed in relief, but Felix's expression did not change. Her anxiety flickered. "So, what does that mean?"

"It means that if I need to leave Civim, you'll have to come with me. This will interrupt your studies. It also means that you might have to go to places you would rather not."

Emya knew that she should be more concerned, but her insides bubbled rather pleasantly at this news. Lydia could never be so close to him.

"I knew the Companion would not easily give up its secrets. Keeping you and me safe and alive is a necessary hindrance."

Her pleasant feelings returned again to anxiety. Connection to Felix via an evil object was not an enviable state, no matter how much she desired it.

"In light of that revelation, I was wondering if you could help us out with some experiments tonight," Felix asked.

Elated by the prospect, Emya replied, "Yes, I'll help however I can."

Her heart soared with the prospect of freedom from the object and a night alone with Felix.

"Great." Felix smiled, suddenly he looked as giddy as she felt. "Come to the State House at eight. Someone will show you to my office."

"Alright," she said.

The day passed too slowly, but her ability to pay attention to her lessons improved significantly. Emya was eager to show Felix that she had been working hard, and she hoped she was now knowledgeable enough to help. Though she doubted the building magic she was practicing in Mistress Lo's lessons would be much use that evening, she applied herself to her studies all the same.

"Excellent work." Mistress Lo examined the white stones she was transforming into basic shapes. It surprised her how easily constructive magic came to her, but the rest of her classmates were not faring so well. Emya had managed to turn the stones into a pyramid, sphere, and had nearly completed her work on a cylinder. Evris, who had achieved a nearly perfect cube and a lumpy sphere, looked on enviously.

"Have you performed magic like this before?" asked Mistress Lo.

"No, Mistress Lo." The Kings had talked about teaching her how to make things with magic—'constructive magic' she now knew it was called—but had never gotten around to it. They probably never intended to.

"Well, very nice work," she said and turned her attention to another pupil. "Mr. Zor, what shape do you call that exactly?"

Emya and Evris went to dinner later than usual, as Evris had convinced Emya to take a trip with her down to the third level to visit Rob. The farm rings were impressive. They were filled with fields of every edible plant Emya knew, and many she did not. The soil never lacked nutrients and an elaborate, magic irrigation system ensured that the soil always had the ideal amount of water. Rob showed them around, explaining the magical aspects that made the farms exceptional.

It was growing dark by the time they climbed the long staircases to the first level. Emya ate quickly and hurried along to the State House, arriving almost half an hour early. She wavered at the entrance, wondering if she ought to wait until the time he was expecting her or just go in. She didn't want to interrupt important work but at least she could let him know she had arrived.

Inside, the magnificent foyer was deserted. Felix had said someone would show her the way to his office, but what if they had all left already? What was she to do if no one came? Deciding it wouldn't hurt to wander around a little, she set off down a long hallway. If she ran into someone she would ask for his office. If she didn't and couldn't find the office, she would go back to the foyer.

The soles of her shoes tapped softly on the floor and reverberated off the stone walls of the deserted hallways. She was just about to backtrack to the foyer when she rounded a corner and heard voices coming from an open door. A gentle, warm breeze flowed over her as she approached. As she came upon the doorway, a horrifyingly familiar sight met her eyes.

He was limply draped over a chair. His arms hung loosely over the armrests and his head drooped against his chest. A shimmering, clear substance oozed from Felix onto the floor. Master Trevylin sat cross-legged at the foot of Felix's chair, his eyes shut, the Companion cradled in his arms. Next to him, Master Kyn traced symbols in the fluid.

Felix opened his eyes. She could sense him through the object and knew that he could feel her too. His lips parted, a silent 'no' escaped them. Emya fled. Through the halls and out into the night, she sprinted through the nearly deserted streets. The orange light of the streetlamps was reminiscent of the dreamscape of her village the night before she witnessed the same scene all those months ago in the throne room.

She fled from the third ring to the second then to the first ring. There, the arch rose before her. A rough hand caught her there and jerked her to a stop. Panicked, Emya whirled, striking her assailant in the chest while she tugged and twisted her arm. Another arm wrapped around her, this one pinning her arms and trapping her in a tactical embrace. Hot tears escaped as she relented and started to sob.

"I warned you about this," Artyem said irritably. "I told you that I didn't want to find you dead on the mountain, yet here you are running off."

He loosened his grip and ran his hand through her hair in long, soothing strokes.

"What happened?" he asked, the ire gone from his voice. He sounded more tired than she felt. She shook her head and then buried it in his chest.

"I have orders to bring you back to the State House," Artyem said.

"No!" she screeched violent tremors shook her to the core.

"From Felix," he added. "He's anxious to explain himself. Which is unusual, as he never feels the need to explain himself to anyone."

Artyem was trying to cheer her up and lighten the mood, but Felix wasn't who she was fleeing.

"Come on." He took her by the arm and marched her back to the State House. Hanging her head in defeat, she let him lead her. Assumptions and implications passed through her mind faster than she could analyze them. If Master Kyn and the others wanted to use the object to take the magic from the mages living in Civim, they certainly possessed that capability now. They must have coerced Felix into telling them how, or perhaps they tricked him. He would not have told them willingly if he knew they were planning to take his magic.

Either way, she was sure that they would do it quickly. They'd drain the magic from one person after another before the other mages realized what was happening. Or perhaps would they drain each of them one at a time, slowly drawing it out as the Kings had. They could add to their power in silence without ever being discovered by the rest of the Citadel. Then she had a disturbing thought. Was Felix their victim or was he part of it?

Had Felix shown them how it worked with the understanding that he would receive part of the power? No. He wouldn't. He couldn't.

Trembling violently, she climbed the steps of the State House. In the foyer Felix was pacing. The two other Masters stood as still as statues. Felix's head jerked up as she entered. He strode over to her with an expression pained with worry.

"Emya, I'm so sorry," he said. "I didn't mean for you to see that. Let me explain."

Artyem let go of her but stood in the doorway, blocking escape. Emya glanced around, looking at Felix and the stone-faced Masters. One thought prevailed over all the others.

"What are you going to do with me?" she whispered.

"Nothing," Felix said helplessly. "I know what it looked like, but I can see trying to convince you otherwise would be fruitless."

"So allow us to make the attempt," Master Kyn said as he stepped forward. "We are not monsters, nor shall we use the object to hurt anyone. We are only trying to understand it. Won't you come with us so we can show you?"

Reluctantly she nodded and followed them down the hall to a parlor. She was glad that they hadn't taken her to the same room she had found them in.

Master Kyn indicated for her to take a seat in a plush gray chair. Master Trevylin handed her a cup of steaming tea, which she took gingerly. Emya hadn't seen where he had gotten it and that did nothing to endear her to them. She took a fortifying sip anyway.

"Felix told us about the men who held him captive, the ones who took his magic by using this object," Master Kyn explained. "When you walked in on us, he knew you would make a run for it. Felix told us how the object tethers you, we immediately contacted Artyem to intercept you before you reached beyond the object's limit."

Startled, Emya nearly spilled the tea as she realized she'd forgotten all about her connection to the

Companion. So long as Felix was here, she could not leave the Citadel, regardless of what nefarious plots the Masters had. Not unless she could take the Companion from them, and that was unlikely.

"They were not taking my magic," Felix said gently. "We need to understand how the object works, and using it seems to be the only way we can learn about it."

"We have subjected it to other tests," said Master Kyn. "We did not want to weaken Felix needlessly and we do not wish to hinder his recovery."

Felix gave an involuntary shudder but spoke in a friendly tone. "I permitted them to do it. It was an experiment."

"Now that you know how to use it," Emya murmured. "What's to stop you?"

"Nothing," Felix said. He was growing impatient. "There was nothing to stop them from taking it by force and draining both of us of our magic, but they haven't and they won't."

Felix took her hands in one of his and with the other tilted her chin up, forcing her to look him in the eye. "You have to trust me now. You have no other choice until I can release us from the Companion. After that, if you want to leave and never return, you can. You have my word."

She nodded, conceding defeat at least for the time being. Felix stepped back, visibly relieved.

"I'm sorry you saw that. I was going to tell you about

it, but I didn't want you to see," he said. "Do you still want to help me tonight? I understand if you'd rather not."

Emya took a fortifying gulp of her tea, which was still the perfect temperature. She glanced at the two Masters who were watching her with a mixture of apprehension and concern. Then she met Felix's sorrowful gaze. Something stirred inside her. They were not quite the feelings she'd had the night before. They were pleasant in a strange way that was familiar but unknowable. It passed as quickly as it came, and she put it aside.

"What is it you need me to do?" she said.

Felix relaxed, visibly relieved. "I think you'll find this very interesting."

Master Kyn took a seat between her and Felix. Master Trevylin sat across from him, gripping the Companion in his hands. Black as onyx, it seemed even more menacing in his clutches. Trevylin, catching her gaze, deliberately handed it to Felix.

"Have you noticed any unusual feelings or thoughts? They might feel like they're not quite your own," Felix said.

That was exactly what she'd been feeling lately. It was exactly what she felt moments ago. Felix read it on her face.

"I thought so," Felix said. "You've been feeling some of my emotions. And we've been sharing some thoughts, though I'm not sure we've always realized it. Remember back on the mountain when we were both thinking about how the Companion might affect you?"

"Yes," Emya said.

"Well, I've been studying the connection between the two of us, which is different from the connection between each of us and the object, but it's difficult to do on my own. I was hoping you'd help me with some experimental spells to see if we can understand it better. Maybe it can help us break the connection."

"Alright," Emya said. "But I don't see how I can help with any spells. We haven't learned any yet. Just regular magic."

Spells, like the one used to create the messenger stones, were intricate and more structured methods of magic designed to cause a specific and consistent result. They were incredibly difficult to do according to Mistress Lo.

"I'll be doing the spell. You know enough to do what I need you to do, but I'm afraid I have to ask you to deviate from the Citadel-approved methods to make up for the gap in your experience. You're going to have to feel this one out," Felix said.

"Feel it out?" Emya asked.

"It's a colloquial phrase among the mages here in Civim referring to filling in knowledge gaps by using the instinct that comes with having the ability to use magic," Master Trevylin supplied. "It is frowned upon when you

145

first begin to learn, but as you advance it becomes more necessary."

"Alright," Emya said indifferently. She didn't trust them any more than the Kings at that moment, so what did it matter whose method she used? Seeing Felix look at her with such anxiousness softened her. "What do you want me to do?"

Felix smiled sheepishly. "It's going to sound a little silly."

She cocked her head and narrowed her eyes. Something inside her squirmed.

"See, right there." He pointed emphatically. "You felt it."

The Masters watched on with interest but said nothing.

"Felt what?" asked Emya.

"Apprehension," said Felix.

"Yes."

"What you just said would have caused her to feel apprehension," said Master Trevylin.

"Yes, but I'd bet it didn't feel quite like her own. Am I right?" he asked Emya. It had been a strange feeling. To say that it was not quite her own seemed a good description, but at the same time, it didn't feel like anyone else's.

"Maybe," she said. Felix's face fell a little but then became determined.

"Well, we'll see after my experiment. As I was

saying, this is a little awkward to ask, but have you been having any strong feelings towards me since last night?"

Heat rushed to her cheeks. Stammering, she tried to come up with an answer that didn't mortify her in front of the prestigious Masters. Failing, she buried her face in her hands.

"Ah, yes, well I thought so." Felix sounded embarrassed but not nearly as much as her. "I'm sorry about that. I was testing my hypothesis and I wanted to make it a pleasant experience for you. I didn't want you to hate me."

"I think you may have failed in that endeavor despite your efforts," Trevylin said.

"I'm sorry, Emya," Felix said sincerely. "Please let me explain."

"She hasn't left in disgust," said Master Trevylin when Emya didn't respond. "Get on with it."

"I've had a feeling for some time that our emotions are affecting each other through the object. I was anxious on the day we arrived. I thought it was because I was still coming to terms with what happened to me, but it seemed to culminate shortly before you met with the Masters. It went away just before you came to visit me and when I saw that you were much calmer than I expected you to be, I was significantly more at peace than I'd been for some time."

"So, you're saying I was making you upset because of the magic that affected my emotion?" Emya asked, guilt washing over her. She quickly pushed the feeling down. She knew this wasn't her fault and that the guilt really should be upon Felix.

"Actually, I think I was upsetting *you*," he said as he slouched in his chair. His gaze drifted across the room. "You shouldn't have been affected so strongly by the magic here."

Silence fell over the room as he sat, contemplating. The Masters watched him with concern but said nothing. A strange, fearful look twitched across his features. For a moment he looked so fragile that one wrong word could shatter him. She knew he was recollecting some horrific memory of his time in captivity. After another moment, his face relaxed into a pleasant smile.

"I'm sorry about that, too. Of course, I had to study the object a little before I could start my experiment, and all day today I have been monitoring myself." He shifted uncomfortably. "It seems that our feelings can compound. When you feel something strongly enough, it transfers over to me, increases, and transfers back to you where it increases yet again. As a result, the anxiety you had from your first day here transferred to me, increased, and then returned to you. This amplification continued until the feelings changed. This only seems to happen when the emotion is too strong to ignore. Yesterday I started an experiment with myself and, just as I suspected, I haven't been able to get you out of my head all day."

He grinned in an attempt to make the situation humorous. Emya scowled as realization struck. The kiss on her hand. That was the experiment. Anger flared inside her with such ferocity that Felix flinched.

"I haven't been able to concentrate on my lessons all day," she said, straining to keep her voice level.

Felix rubbed his face, groaning. "I'm sorry. Truly I am. But this is important. This could be the key to separation. I had to test it, and if I'd told you what I was doing it might not have worked."

As quickly as it flared, Emya's anger burned out. She wanted to be freed. Whatever aided with that must be endured. "How does this help us?"

Felix stood up and motioned for her to follow him. Then he sat cross-legged on the floor in front of the window and motioned for her to sit with him.

"Emotion is connected to magic. This phenomenon we're experiencing is a symptom of what the object is doing to us," he explained. "I need to find out what that is."

Master Kyn handed the object to him. "We'll be back. Be careful."

"We will," Felix said.

He and Master Trevylin left the room.

"Now," Felix said as he placed the object on the floor between them. "Remember how it felt when you connected with the object?"

Emya nodded, acutely aware of how pleasant it

was to be so close to him. She tried to push that feeling down but could not. Was this because it wasn't quite her feeling?

"I need you to do what you did that first time the companion tried to take your power. I'm going to try and take your power. I won't actually," he added at the alarm he saw on her face. "It shouldn't be difficult to resist. Are you ready?"

She nodded again and Felix took both her hands, bowed his head, and closed his eyes. The object's embedded gems began to swirl in their sockets and for the second time, she felt it pull at her magic, though this time wasn't nearly as strong as the first. Instead, it felt as though someone was gently tugging at her. She resisted as she had before and the tugging stopped.

Felix lifted his head, opening his eyes. "You're pretty strong. Master Kyn had mentioned that you were powerful. I can see that he was not exaggerating."

"I don't feel powerful," she mumbled shyly, though she couldn't hide a little pleased smile.

"You will after more training. Let's keep going." He took a deep breath as if to steel himself to do something unpleasant. "I'm going to do that again. Are you ready?"

"Yes," she said.

"Good. And I'm sorry about this in advance."

Emya braced, expecting pain. Felix leaned forward, wrapped one hand around her hair, and pressed his lips against hers.

Surprise and delight filled Emya at the same time as she felt the tug at her power. It was the easiest thing in the world to break its grip. Felix leaned back and then stood, leaving Emya on the floor in a slight daze. He paced back and forth while she got her erratically beating heart under control.

"Did it work?" she asked once she found her voice.

"Yes," he said absently, lost in thought.

"So?"

"I discovered something that I didn't expect," he said. He stopped pacing and stood in front of her. "I'm sorry."

"You already said that before you kissed me," Emya said.

Red filled his cheeks; he rubbed his hands over his face, mortified. "I know. I'm sorry about what I found. I can't separate us from the object. It's clear to me now that there is no way to do it."

"We're stuck like this?" she asked.

"For now. There might still be a way to free us, but it would be very specific. We'd have to figure out who created the object and see if they created a way to remove it. And while that is possible, finding that information may not be."

"Is that what you didn't expect?"

"No. I think the object may be giving us more magic. I'm not sure where the magic is coming from though, and I can't tell if this is by design. It's such a minuscule amount it's almost incidental."

"Is the object taking magic from someone else?"

"I don't know. Maybe. But it's just the two of us in here. There is any number of magical sources in this building alone for it to draw magic from. We'll have to do an investigation. If the companion is weakening the citadel's magical protections, that could be very bad."

"You said it was only a little."

"Only a little is transferred to us, but the amount siphoned off by the object could be much greater. This thing leaks raw magic like a broken dam when you use it to transfer magic to someone who isn't connected. It's very inefficient."

Felix took a deep breath and let out a long sigh. Ambling back to her, he held out his hand and pulled her to her feet. She swayed slightly, giddy from the magic and the kiss. He steadied her with a hand on her back but pulled it away quickly.

"Are you okay?" he asked.

"Yes, I'll be fine."

The door creaked open and Master Kyn poked his head in.

"Is everything alright?" he asked.

"Yes, Master Kyn," said Felix. "We've just finished."

Master Kyn turned his assessing gaze to Emya, who gazed back tiredly. All the feeling had drained from her, leaving nothing but a desire to sleep.

"Why don't you take Emya to bed and we'll discuss

what you found after? Unless you'd like to stay," Kyn said to Emya. She shook her head. The Masters bid her goodnight and Felix led her out into the cool mountain air.

He walked her back to her room, leaving her at the door just as he had the night before. This time there was no grand gesture, only an apologetic smile through his troubled expression and a wish goodnight.

Evris was sitting on her bed reading a large, old book when Emya came in. She looked eager to ask questions, but when she saw the look on Emya's face she sighed.

"What happened?" she asked gently. Emya shook her head and fell onto her bed, burying her face in the pillow.

"Are you alright?" Evris asked.

Emya nodded.

"Can't tell me or don't want to?"

Emya rolled over and sat up with a deep sigh.

"I can't tell you," she said. "But I wish I could. I don't know what to think."

"Surely there is something you can tell me without giving away the secret."

Emya thought about it. As long as she didn't mention the Companion she could tell Evris.

"He wanted me to help him with some magic. I was helping him with an experiment concerning the relationship between emotion and magic."

Evris nodded.

"So, he had you do magic with emotion?"

"Yes."

"Is that what's bothering you?"

"No," Emya buried her face in her hands, muffling her words. "He kissed me."

Evris's jaw dropped. She gaped at Emya in utter surprise until her face twisted into a triumphant grin.

"I knew it! I knew he liked you."

Emya peeked through her fingers. "What do you mean? What made you think that?"

"It was painfully obvious the way he always tried to be near you during the trek up the mountain, or how he took care of you after you fell, but mainly it was the infatuation on his face every time he looked at you. I saw it the first time I saw you two together during dinner at my house."

"I don't know about that," Emya said.

Emya knew that the Companion didn't create emotions. Felix probably felt some affection for her because she helped him escape the Kings. Maybe Evris was mistaking that for infatuation. He had been incredibly grateful to be saved from that living death.

"Trust me. I've devoted most of my life to ascertaining who's in love with who in my village. It's my favorite pastime. So, what did you do? Kiss him back? Slap him?"

Emya gave a short bark of surprised laughter. It hadn't occurred to her to slap him, but now it seemed like a missed opportunity.

"Neither. It was part of the magic. Strong emotions." Emya got up and busied herself with getting ready for bed, hiding her blushing face with her back to Evris.

"I don't know how I feel about that. That's not very romantic, is it? Did you like it?"

"No."

"Why not? Was he a bad kisser?" Evris stopped and inhaled sharply. Then she asked in a low voice, "Was that your first kiss?"

"Yes," Emya admitted. "And I didn't like it because he surprised me. And it wasn't because he wanted to, it was for the spell, and, well, other reasons too."

"Ah, okay. That would bother me too. But if he'd kissed you because he wanted to, would you have liked it then?"

Emya wasn't sure how to answer. She didn't know what to make of any of it, but at least she now knew the difference between the feelings Felix was projecting and her own. She felt an undeniable affection for him after all they'd been through.

"Maybe," she said. "If I knew he wanted to, I might know if I wanted to."

Evris grinned. "He wants to, I'm sure. You'll see."

Chapter Seven

A good night's sleep, a long, soothing bath, and a hearty breakfast did not lift Emya's spirits as much as she'd hoped. She was still unsure if she was more bothered by Felix's manipulation or the reality that he couldn't find a way to separate them from the object. Emya didn't notice the whispers around her on the way to breakfast until Evris huffed angrily and shot a dirty look past Emya that she at first thought was meant for her

"Sorry. I'm not feeling myself," Emya said.

"What?" Evris said, confused.

"Aren't you mad at me?" Emya asked.

"No. I'm mad at those two." She inclined her head towards a point behind Emya. A glance over her shoulder confirmed her sudden suspicion. Sitting with their heads together were the two girls who had confronted her in the alley.

"What did they do?" Emya asked.

"It's what they're doing, still!" Evris threw her hands up and sighed angrily. "They're spreading rumors about you. I've heard them and I won't stand for it. I'm going to knock their heads together if they don't stop."

With a jolt, Emya realized she hadn't told Evris about her unfortunate encounter with those girls. Evris had no idea that Arteym had rescued her. In a low voice, as they worked together on a project Master Nikola had set them, she related the tale.

"So that's why Artyem was with you and Felix at dinner. I wondered," Evris said. "But that's terrible! Why would they spread such nasty rumors? You haven't done anything, and if anyone would get to know you they'd know that none of those rumors are true."

"I suppose I don't let them get to know me."

"Oh please. I got to know you easily. Why is everyone else so bad at making friends?"

Emya laughed. She was once again so glad that Evris was her friend.

"Anyway. What should we do about those girls? I don't want them spreading any more rumors."

"Nothing. Artyem says people don't believe them. They'll stop when they realize no one is listening."

Evris looked skeptical.

"If all they were doing was spreading rumors, I'd agree. But I overheard them. They were talking about ways they could force you to show your true intentions."

"My true intentions are to learn magic and not make any trouble, I don't see a problem with that."

"Emya," Evris said seriously. "The point isn't your intentions; the point is what they might do to you."

Emya sighed, apprehension growing within her. She couldn't guess what the girls might try but it was bound to be dreadful if they perceived her as a real threat. Once again, Emya withdrew into herself, though she tried to behave as though nothing was wrong for Evris's sake. They joked flippantly about invoking the wrath of Felix and Artyem if anyone tried to hurt Emya, and how the quarrelsome friends would probably get distracted squabbling with each other while Emya was dragged away by an angry mob. That made Emya laugh, but as they walked to lunch, she became soberly aware of the small group of girls that were whispering behind them. Evris pointedly wrapped her arm through Emya's and led her ahead.

At lunch, Emya received a very unexpected surprise. Lydia plopped her plate angrily across from Evris and Emya, followed by Runel and Rob.

"Do you know what they're saying about you, Emya?" Lydia said bluntly. "I can't imagine that you're unaware of it."

"I know," Emya said softly. "I thought everyone

knew."

"No. It's been circulating among the younger mages, but they've been trying to keep it from spreading through the Citadel," Runel said darkly. "They don't want us older students or the Masters to find out."

"They think they know better than us. They know they'll get in a lot of trouble if we find out whatever they're planning," Runel said testily.

"And they *will* get in trouble," Lydia added fiercely. "The Masters are rounding up the usual troublemakers as we speak."

"What we're trying to say," Runel said carefully seeing Emya's confused expression, "is you can tell us when something is bothering you. We're your friends, Emya."

Though it hadn't felt like they were her friends, that was her own failing she decided. She accepted the declaration at face value.

"Thanks," she said. "How did you find out?"

"Felix," Rob said. "He was in the garden with the Masters and he started asking me about you. Wanted to know if I knew what was going on. He's livid."

"He should be. Accusing someone of being like that girl without a shred of evidence is absolutely abhorrent," said Lydia. "I can't believe he let it go this far."

"He wasn't here when that happened," Runel reminded her.

Rob nodded. "Which is why I told him to let us

take care of it. He's got enough to worry about with the gardens right now."

"What's wrong with the gardens?" Evris asked.

"Oh," Rob said. He looked extremely troubled. "Some of the magic has, well, gone wrong."

"Gone rotten more like," Runel said.

"Does that happen often?" asked Evris.

"No. It can, but it's incredibly rare. It's usually because two kinds of magic react poorly when used in conjunction or even too close together, but there is nothing in a garden that could have caused it. We're at a loss."

They continued to discuss this subject, with Evris asking questions about how magic interacts. By the look on her face, they had some really interesting answers but Emya wasn't listening. Instead, her mind pondered the stint of insanity that had swept through her village before she left. It certainly matched the description of 'rotten magic', but was it a coincidence that the Companion had been there and it was now in Civim?

"I hope it doesn't affect our lesson with Mistress Lo," Evris said. "We're starting the basics of natural magic and we're supposed to start in the garden."

"I don't think it will," said Rob. "The rot is only in one section of the gardens. It happens I'm going to be there for that class. Mistress Lo wants me to do a demonstration."

Evris squealed in delight. Emya, also interested in

seeing Rob's talent in action, set aside her worry and joined the conversation.

After lunch, they joined the rest of their classmates at the entrance of the gardens. Rob, having walked over with them, went to stand next to Mistress Lo, who introduced him and then motioned for the students to follow him.

The day was clear and cool, though the sun provided enough warmth that Emya wasn't chilled. Flanked on both sides by fragrant, beautiful flowers and plants, Emya settled into a dreamy sense of peace.

They stopped in a small grove of budding trees. Rob demonstrated simple magic by healing dying branches and coaxing the flowers into bloom. He even demonstrated how to make fruit grow within seconds. Emya watched it all through a growing haze. His words were muted, and she began to sway. It was only then that she realized there was a problem, but it was too late.

"Emya!" Evris called in a muffled voice as the world went black around her.

~~*~*~*~*

She wasn't sure if she was dreaming, but it was impossible that she was awake. The wind gusted around her in the Citadel garden, snapping and stinging with energy. The mages who had been there moments

161

ago were gone and the garden was filled with her old neighbors. She knew that they couldn't be there; they would never come to a place filled with magic.

She couldn't quite see them though. They were too far away. She ran into the garden, but the villagers moved away from her as she advanced. All she could make out was the blurry outline of strangely clad men and women. Emya's legs grew heavy, each step was like lifting a boulder. As she passed through the phoenix grove, Felix appeared with Evris, Artyem, and a strange regal man who she didn't know. He stood out sharp and clear in contrast to her friends.

She called out each of their names, but none acknowledged her. They wore the same strange clothes as the villagers, but as she finally drew near she saw that they were not clothes, but rather snaking, choking vines wrapped all around them. Wide-eyed and pleading, they watched her, silent and immobile. Emya tore at the vines to no avail. The man she didn't know opened his mouth to speak, but no sound came out.

An earsplitting cry pierced the air. Dark shadows circled above them and then they dived, snatching up the bound villagers. A shadow creature, as large as a house, dove towards them, blocking all light. Emya screamed.

~~*~*~*~*

Emya lay in a semi-conscious state, aware that the dream had ended but unable to bring herself to full wakefulness. Gradually the sounds of the world coaxed her out of sleep.

"I don't know what it could have been. We weren't doing any magic at the time." Mistress Lo was speaking.

"I think we can rule out conflicting magic from other students," spoke Felix's soft voice, full of concern. "I have a feeling I know what caused this."

Emya pried her eyes open. Encompassing her vision was Felix's face, twisted in a grim expression, though it immediately softened into relief when he saw she was awake.

"Hey, look who's back," he said lightly. Emya blinked as she looked around. The light, blinding at first, dimmed and revealed the healer's room. Beneath her was a soft bed. She felt like jelly.

"How are you feeling?" Felix asked.

Emya groaned weakly, too disoriented to speak. She couldn't shake the sense of terror the dream had evoked. Something was going to happen. She could feel it in her pounding heart. Felix studied her, worrying his lip.

"Something's wrong," he said to Mistress Haven as she placed a warm hand on Emya's clammy forehead and slid it over her eyes. A pleasant tingling sensation started at the back of her eyes and spread through the rest of her head.

"Yes," Mistress Haven concluded as she removed her hand. "There is something that holds influence over her thoughts. Something outside of her. I haven't encountered anything quite like it in a long time."

"Ah," said Felix, chagrined. "I'm aware of that. I meant she looks upset."

Mistress Haven gave him a condescending look. "And you're sure a perception-bending parasitic magic doesn't have anything to do with it?"

"Fair point. Wait." His eyes widened with sudden fear. "Perception-bending?"

"Yes."

"Can you elaborate?"

Mistress Haven considered the question for a moment, her fingers tapping absently on the headboard of Emya's bed.

"Something is impacting her senses, though I don't think it's strong enough to overcome her while she's awake, it might cause strange, vivid dreams. They may feel like reality to her."

"Is that it?" Felix turned his intense gold eyes to Emya's. "Did you have an upsetting dream?"

She nodded and shuddered. Felix brushed her hair back soothingly.

"She needs to rest," said Mistress Haven. "After a day and night in bed with a few of my special remedies she will be well."

Felix nodded and took Emya's hand, squeezing it

gently.

"You hear that?" he said. "Rest up. I'll come talk to you in the morning."

Emya clutched his hand as he pulled it away. Ever practical, she knew her dream was just that, but deep in her instinctive, animalistic core, she needed to be protected, and Felix was the only one she trusted to do that. This was far too much to explain to him when she couldn't summon her voice, but maybe he would stay for a little while.

With a soft sigh, he sat back down, still holding her hand.

"Please tell Master Kyn I'll be a little longer. Then send a message to Artyem to meet me in two hours," he said to Mistress Lo. She nodded and strolled purposefully out. It was a little disconcerting for Emya to see her teacher taking orders from Felix so dutifully.

After a few minutes of laying quietly, Emya got her breathing under control and her heart stopped hammering.

"Why do you need to see Artyem?" she asked Felix.

"Hm? Oh. Some new mages have been found in a kingdom not too far from here. He's being sent to escort them, but I need to talk to him before he goes."

"Talk about what?"

"Nothing you need to worry about," he reassured her.

Feeling stronger, she pushed herself up a little.

"I don't like this," she said, her voice filled with anguish. She felt as though a great weight was crushing her. Felix sagged in his chair and rubbed his face with his free hand.

"I'm sorry," he said. "I know it's been tough. I haven't made anything easier for you either. I understand if you want to leave Civim. I can make arrangements."

Emya silenced him with a wave of her hand. "That's not what I meant."

She felt as though they were running out of time. She knew that something was coming and she needed Felix to listen.

"I had a nightmare," she explained, "but it felt real, more real than any dream I have ever had except one."

She explained the dream she had back at her village and then the dream she'd just had. Felix listened with interest and a little confusion.

When she finished, he crossed his arms and peered up at the ceiling for a few minutes, thinking.

"Magic can affect dreams," he said at last. "But not in any way that we understand. Some mages are what you might call 'seers,' or ones that can have dreams depicting the future. Though it's often extremely difficult to determine if they're really having visions or if they're just guessing based on limited possible outcomes. If I recall correctly, there have only been two mages in all recorded history who are considered legitimate seers. Both of their visions were specific, detailed, and accurate. Even then, those visions were few and far between. Decades."

"I don't think these are visions of the future," Emya said with a sudden realization. "I think they are visions of what is already happening."

Felix cocked his head quizzically at her.

"When I had the first dream," she explained, "my neighbors were already acting strangely, and it got worse, as I dreamed it would, but already things were in motion. As if I realized it in my dream before I realized it in real life. Does that make sense?"

Felix nodded. "I see what you mean. The question is—"

"Is the Companion causing this?" she said, finishing his thought for him. He smiled.

"Exactly. The answer, of course, is most likely yes. Even so, I don't think it's something you need worry about."

"Not any more than I need to worry about whatever else it's doing to me," she added bitterly.

"About that. I think it might have been my fault that you passed out. I was experimenting to see if I could understand where the Companion siphoned magic from and I may have accidentally dropped it beyond the allowable distance for you. Sorry."

Surprising even herself, Emya curled over her knees, laughing. Startled, Felix put a hand on her back in concern. She looked up, meeting his worried eyes with hers crinkled in mirth.

"What's so funny?" he asked with a confused smile.

"I thought it was something serious," she said through laughter. "But no. You... You dropped it."

She bent over in a fit of uncontrollable giggling. It was so ridiculous. This was the last thing she would have expected. She had collapsed over nothing more than the smallest mistake. "Your butterfingers could have killed me! What if you dropped it off a cliff or into a swift river?"

"It wasn't like that," he said, grinning sheepishly. "But I see what you mean."

Gradually her laughter wore out and she lay down, tired, but feeling much better.

"I'd better go now," Felix said. "I have to talk to Kyn."

He stood up and ran his fingers through his hair. Emya glimpsed the window behind him as a great black shadow obscured the streetlamps.

Glass shattered, spraying over them. A winged creature, larger than a man, forced itself through the window, its neck stretched out and a flat, square mouth of jagged teeth snapped at them. Felix darted out of range as its jaw almost closed over his leg. He grabbed Emya by the arm as she struggled out of the bed, glass piercing her hands and feet. He pulled her towards the door just as the creature squeezed into the room. In the foyer Mistress Haven tottered out of her office, her face as white as a sheet.

"Out!" Felix yelled, shoving the door open. They stumbled into the night. The creature screeched and snapped, its maw pressing out of the door as it tore at the wall behind them.

Felix pulled Emya through the courtyard outside the healing house. Huge shadows swooped above them, screeching and diving at panicking mages. Children scrambled for safety in the towers. The adults aimed crackling and sparking bursts of energy at the beasts. A battle shouldn't be so beautiful, she thought vaguely as they ducked a bolt of energy that rippled just over their heads. Felix defended her as they ran through the streets, blasting shadow after shadow with bursts of light. Blue, red, and gold lighting shot from Felix's frantically waving hand. No, not his hand exactly, but forming in the air in front of them then directed by a push or pull.

The narrow paths bottlenecked the creatures above them yet fewer mages could help Felix fight them off. More and more shadows clawed their way down into the streets until they ran into a small shopping square swarming with the creatures. Trapped and cut off from all the other mages they stopped. Felix fought furiously, lighting up the rapidly shrinking space between them with hot, hissing magic. The air burned with scalding, rushing air as magically charged wind clashed with the cool night. Felix would soon be overwhelmed.

Emya ducked as one of the creatures dodged a blast

from Felix and swooped over him. Its claws grazed the small of her back, before it tumbled to the ground. Felix directed a blast that hit it square in the chest. It burst into a cloud of black mist. Emya crouched behind Felix, making herself as small as possible. She screamed as two creatures flew at them, but her panic alerted Felix just in time to blast them to bits. The creatures were closing in on them.

Like a hole punched through paper, lights penetrated the shadows. The creatures began to disperse, some taking to the sky while others disintegrated into nothing. As Felix's strength failed and he collapsed to his knees, the battling mage broke through the shadows. Felix managed to produce a magical barrier, protecting them both until the rest of the creatures were driven away by the mages.

A wall of mages closed in around them. Master Kyn lumbered out of the crowd. He was flanked by Mistress Tunin and Master Noah.

Master Kyn gazed down at them wearily.

"Are you alright?" Master Noah asked as he helped Felix to his feet. Mistress Tunin tugged Emya up and gently pried her grip off of Felix's arm. Breathing heavily, Felix nodded and gave them a thumbs up. A punch-drunk grin spread across his face.

"I haven't fought that hard," he said breathlessly, "since my last Star Night."

"That's right," Master Noah said, leading him away

through the crowd. Mistress Tunin followed with Emya. "You keep up that spirit."

Most of the mages were busy assessing the damage or talking to one another, but a few watched silently and grim-faced as Emya and Felix were led away by the Masters. Emya wondered what sort of gossip would be spreading by the next morning. To her surprise, she spotted Runel, Lydia, and Rob among the crowd watching them go. They looked pale and worried but not injured she was relieved to find.

Emya hadn't expected to see anyone she knew among the fighters, though looking around she realized there were too few Masters to take on such a numerous force. There was no one as young as her among them, she was relieved to find. She hoped that meant Evris was safe. Seemingly everyone was up and about. Only a few sat on the cobbled walk, tending injuries. That didn't mean no one had been carried off.

Having lost all track of where she was, Emya was surprised to be led up the steps of the State House. They climbed up the stairs to the top level. Emya was panting by the time they entered a large, dim room with tables covered in books, maps, and thick rolls of parchment. The walls were adorned with large slabs of a dull black stone that had been sanded down to a smooth surface. These stones were covered in illegible chalk writing and perplexing diagrams. Mistress Tunin guided her to a plush chair and pushed her gently into it. Felix took a seat across from her. Master Noah stood over a table, scrutinizing a complex and detailed map. Master Kyn stood across the room and stared out the window. No one said anything. Emya caught Felix's eye with a small smile, though he was struggling to keep his eyes open.

After a few minutes, the doors opened and the rest of the Masters filed in. Each looked wearied and distressed.

"Alright," said Master Nikola with grim humor as he sauntered in. "Who summoned the Dashna? I know it was one of you." He drew his accusing finger around the room, pointing at each of them.

"We know who it was, Nikola," Felix said with a mischievous smile. "Emya, of course."

Too tired to be upset, Emya shrugged weakly. "Must be."

"We'll address that in a moment," Master Kyn said softly. He appeared particularly disturbed, dark, purple skin lined his eyes and he rubbed his forehead frequently as though it pained him. "First, give me your reports."

"All younger students have been reported safe," said Mistress Tunin. "No injuries."

"All adult students are safe too," said Master Nikola. "Several sustained injuries, though nothing too serious."

"All teachers safe," said Master Noah. "No injuries." Emya wondered how he'd managed to check on all the teachers while he was in the room with them the whole time, then she caught sight of the little messenger stone in his hand.

"I should hope not," murmured Mistress Lo. "They should know what they're doing."

"All citizen residents safe," reported a Master Emya did not know. "Though Mistress Gian was found severely injured. She was taken to the infirmary, though the damage and number of injured are making it very difficult for Mistress Haven to do her work. She believes Mistress Gian may have been lifted into the air by the creature and dropped. She expects her to recover, however."

Emya's heart sank. She liked the nice shopkeeper. It was the Companion's presence that had attracted the creatures and by extent her and Felix. If Mistress Gian or anyone had died, she knew it would have been their fault. A glance at Felix told her he felt the same, maybe worse.

"It was not as bad as it could have been," Master Noah said.

"It will only get worse the longer we put off the inevitable," Master Kyn said. "There is no denying that the Companion is responsible for drawing dark forces to Civim."

"True," said Master Noah. "But let's not dismiss the fact that the concentration of magic in Civim has drawn power-seeking foes since its creation. We should not send a powerful object away from our protection simply because it is doing what magic inevitably does."

Shocked though she was to learn that Civim was not as well protected as she thought, Emya was more surprised at the burst of dread inside her at the prospect of being sent away.

Though it was not long ago that she tried to run away, she knew if such a host of creatures attacked her and Felix without the protection of the Civim mages, they would not survive.

"You were right next to me as we fought this night," Master Nikola said fiercely. "Were you blinded by fear? Did you not see what the rest of us saw?"

"Nikola," said Master Kyn, his tone warning.

"I saw," said Master Noah curtly, leaning forward in his chair. "They went straight for Felix and Emya. Every one of them. But that doesn't change the fact that this is the safest place to keep and study the object. This is the reason Civim was created."

"One of the reasons," Mistress Hanna said. "We also have a duty to teach and protect the young mages we bring here, including Emya." She turned and nodded at Emya with a small, encouraging smile.

All attention turned to Emya then. Each of the Masters and Mistresses had expressions that ranged from concern to embarrassment.

Emya glanced at Felix, who was not looking at her but staring irritably at his folded hands in his lap.

"What do you say, Felix?" Master Kyn asked.

"Oh, are you going to listen to me now?" Felix said.

Master Noah grimaced and spoke softly, "You will speak respectfully to Master Kyn."

"He, and the rest of you, have been asking me the same question since I returned. I'll tell you now what I've said since the beginning: If there is no way to subdue it here, and there isn't, then I must go and find one. This object cannot be hidden away as long as it is connected to me or Emya. It will continue to draw enemies. Whether by magical means or by our deaths, the connection between myself, Emya, and this object must be severed."

"I recall what you have said," Master Kyn said deliberately. He folded his hands and put them against his lips. Then he closed his eyes. "My question remains the same: What can you do to ensure Emya's safety once you leave Civim? She must go with you, but we cannot justify sending her on what is surely a fatal errand for one so inexperienced."

Felix crossed his arms and glared out at the floor. Emya guessed, and with their connection, she felt relatively certain of her guess, that he'd been posed this question before and had yet to determine an answer that satisfied himself, let alone the rest of the Masters. It wasn't until then that Emya felt the gravity of the situation. Every moment they were in Civim they put everyone around them in danger. It was likely that they were even harming the other mages as the object siphoned off the magic around it.

"It doesn't matter," Felix said finally. He sent an apologetic glance her way. "There is no way I can assure her protection, but that changes nothing. We must leave."

"You place an impossible burden on him if you continue to insist upon the protection of Emya."

The room's occupants turned in surprise. Just inside the door stood Artyem. He was flanked by two other Tritium guards.

"None of you will be able to protect Emya if that object overwhelms her, yet you insist that Felilx must find a way to do what you cannot? By keeping them here you are putting her in more danger than whatever it will take to sever the connection."

No one corrected him. Felix smiled and held up his hand in a gesture of thanks.

Master Kyn stood up and paced around the room, passing between Emya and Felix, to stare at the chalk diagrams. Everyone waited in silence. Some observed Master Kyn while others stared off into space, lost in their thoughts.

Master Kyn finally turned and sighed heavily.

"It is against my judgment to send Felix away after he was gone so long and considering what he's been through." Felix looked as though he had something to say about that but held his peace as Kyn went on. "Nor do I believe that it is right to allow Emya to go with him, especially given the perils they undoubtedly will face."

The Masters and Mistresses nodded and murmured in agreement.

"The fact, however, is undeniable. Their arrival here was premature. Had they no need of rest and resources, they might not have come here at all. They must go and finish what has been started or they will never be safe, even if they are within our community. There are older places in the world with ancient records that may contain the information they need. Until they sever the connection, neither their safety nor their future can be assured, not even by Civim."

Murmurs of agreement and concession echoed around the room.

"Emya will be safe," Artyem said. "As I will be by her side the entire time."

Felix shot Artyem a scathing look. "I don't remember inviting you along."

"I invited myself before I was volunteered by the council." Artyem nodded towards Master Kyn.

"Your foresight is as sharp as your wit," said Master Noah. "You will be going with them."

"If that's settled," Master Kyn said, "I think we should let Emya and Felix go rest."

Getting to her feet, exhausted and dazed, she took a few swaying steps towards the door before Felix wrapped his arm through hers and led her out. Artyem clapped him on the shoulder as he passed.

Felix did not take her back to her shared room

with Evris, who she hoped was waiting for her, safe and sound, but instead led her to the private houses.

The eighth ring was peaceful and quiet. Dim lamps illuminated the wide slate path between rows of small but charming cottages.

"I think it's best if you stay with me tonight, just in case," he said dubiously as he led her up a pebbly walkway that was flanked by short, perfectly even grass. They took three steps onto a small porch and Felix opened the door.

Emya stepped into the little sitting room already brightly lit with magical lamps. Seated by a roaring fire was Evris. She sprang up with an unintelligible cry of relief and crushed Emya in a hug.

"I'm so glad you're alright. I was so worried!" She stood back, holding Emya at arm's length and examining her. "Are you hurt at all?"

"Not a bit," Emya said, giddy with relief. "Are you?"

"I was running. I fell and scraped up my hands and knees, but Rob was there to help me." She grinned cheekily. Then, remembering Felix was there too, she turned her concern on him. "Are you alright?"

Felix smiled bracingly. "Never better. Good to know I still have it in me to fight off a bunch of demonic monsters."

Evris hugged him too.

"I thought you'd be happier knowing Evris was safe," Felix said to Emya. "I had her brought here for the night.

It will be your first slumber party."

"My what?" Emya had never heard the term.

"Oh don't mind him. Why don't we have something to eat and then go to bed," Evris said. "I assume you have something suitable for a late-night snack?"

They munched on some dried fruit that had been rummaged from Felix's sparsely stocked pantry and washed it down with a glass of chilled elderflower cordial. Then Evris showed Emya to a little room with a bed large enough for two. Felix poked his head in long enough to ask if they needed anything else before he disappeared to somewhere else in the house. Emya suspected he would stay up and plan the journey ahead. Maybe he was making up for all the time he was too weak to do anything because of the Kings, but he was much more active and fidgety than she would have expected. She felt that feeling within him, as she climbed into bed next to Evris. A nagging feeling in the pit of her stomach told her to get up and do something, anything, particularly if it would help separate her from the object. However, as she drifted off, the feeling subsided and she knew Felix was sleeping too.

BIO

As a young girl Amy enjoyed hearing the tales of Redwall and Harry Potter read to her by her mother every night. As a result, she brings her lifelong love of fantasy to life in her writing. With a degree in Molecular Biology she also has a love for science and science fiction. When she is not writing she is knitting, going to the beach, or spending time with her family.